PULP
Literature

PULP
Literature

PULP LITERATURE PRESS

Issue No. 28, Autumn 2020

Publisher: Pulp Literature Press; Managing Editor: Jennifer Landels; Senior Editor: Mel Anastasiou; Acquisitions Editor: Genevieve Wynand; Editor: Jessica Fabrizius; Poetry Editors: Daniel Cowper & Emily Osborne; Assistant Editors: Samantha Olson, Veronica Kos & Melisa Gruger; Copy Editors: Amanda Bidnall & Mary Rykov; Proofreader: Mary Rykov; Graphic Design: Amanda Bidnall; Cover Design: Kate Landels; First Readers: Carol McCauley & Brenda Carre; Advertising: Samantha Olson. For advertising rates, direct inquiries to info@pulpliterature.com.

Cover painting, *The Faery Godmother* by Ashley-Rose Goentoro. Artwork for 'Chimæra' by Weiwei Xu. All other illustrations by Mel Anastasiou.

Pulp Literature: ISSN 2292-2164 (Print), ISSN 2292-2172 (Digital), Issue No. 28, Autumn 2020.

Published quarterly by Pulp Literature Press, 21955 16 Ave, Langley, BC, Canada V2Z IK5, pulpliterature.com, at $15.00 per copy. Annual subscription $50.00 in Canada, $68.00 in continental USA, $86.00 elsewhere. Printed in Victoria, BC, Canada, by First Choice Books / Victoria Bindery. Copyright © 2020 Pulp Literature Press. All stories and works of art copyright © 2020 their authors as per bylines.

Pulp Literature Press gratefully acknowledges the support of the Canada Council for the Arts.

Pulp Literature is a proud member of the Magazine Association of BC and Magazines Canada.

TABLE OF CONTENTS

Origin Stories

My father, born in Germany, immigrated with his family to Canada when he was nine. A childhood friend, born in Canada to Italian parents, moved to Italy when she was twelve. Another, born in India, came to Canada when she was eight. All of them, like so many, lived childhood in one language and later years in another.

Our first language is handed down by our parents. Through it we weave our personal, familial, and cultural narratives. It orients us in time and space; it is a foundation of self. For those with both a mother tongue and a linguistic stepparent, personal and cultural identity might seem to exist in a third space — in a liminal realm of (n)either/(n)or. A singular place where *home* and *away* aren't easily pinned to any map.

The stories in this issue are alive with movement, migration, and memory. Through them we travel through time and space and place. They ask us to consider the limits of location and the challenges of dislocation. And many speak directly to the experience of discontinuity — and discovery — in language and culture.

Since its inception, *Pulp Literature* has been a literary home for many genres. Multiple voices meet and mingle, the familiar and the not-yet-known tucked beneath the same gorgeous cover. Whether in crossing genres or oceans, diverse narratives show us not only what is different, but also what is shared. Whatever one's journey, for a few moments at least, 'You Are Here'.

~Genevieve Wynand

IN THIS ISSUE

Our journey begins under the watchful gaze of *The Faery Godmother* by cover artist **Ashley Rose Goentoro**.

Next we step into the mists of mystery with the genre-blending ghost story 'Man with Golden Helmet' by featured author **Renée Sarojini Saklikar**.

Continuing along, **Dawn Lo** in 'Little Snowflake Girls' and **Weiwei Xu** in 'Chimæra' introduce us to young people exploring meaningful questions of identity and belonging.

Then, like trailside inukshuks, memories pile up and tumble away in 'Moons of Saturn' by **James Dorr**, 'Practising the Art of Forgetting' by **Soramimi Hanarejima**, and 'Starry Nights' by **David Milne**.

And what is a walk in the literary wilds without a cheeky raccoon or the chatter of birds? **AJ Lee**, in 'What Kind of Story', and Magpie winners **Charlene Kwiatkowski**, **Maria Ford**, and **Cara Waterfall** delight with their bewitching words.

Explore solutions to two very different puzzles with **Susan Pieters** in 'Hoax' and SiWC contest winner **Cameron MacDonald** in 'Mourgadze'.

Finally, on journeys of their own, fan favourites Frankie Ray and Toinette return, taking two very different leaps of faith. Whether by way of closet or carriage, keeping safe means keeping up appearances for Frankie Ray in 'The Sleuth with the Platinum Hair' by **Mel Anastasiou** and Toinette in 'The Shepherdess: Versailles' by **JM Landels**.

Pulp Literature Press

Out of the fires of a Caribbean slave revolt, shipwrecked on the jungle coast of 16th-century Ecuador, an educated slave, a shaman, and a monk hunted by the Inquisition fight for freedom against the might of Imperial Spain.

Dive into an epic slipstream novel of intrigue and adventure from fantasy author Matthew Hughes, the writer George R.R. Martin calls 'criminally underrated,' and Robert J. Sawyer says is 'a towering talent.'

'A triumph!' - Cecelia Holland
'Sensational' - Candas Jane Dorsey

pulpliterature.com

Fantastic Fresh Fiction!

PULP Literature

MAN WITH GOLDEN HELMET

Renée Sarojini Saklikar

Renée Sarojini Saklikar (*Surrey Poet Laureate, 2015–2018*) *is the author of three books and six chapbooks. Her work has been adapted for opera and visual art. She teaches creative writing, has judged our Magpie Award for Poetry and is working on a sci-fi epic in verse. 'Man with Golden Helmet' combines two of her favourite genres: ghost stories and memoir.*

ℳAN WITH GOLDEN HELMET

August on a Sunday at the art gallery in the year 2009: the Dutch Masters arrive to this Pacific Northwest place. Outside the gallery façade, huge banners hang, imprinted with colour: the brown and red and gold of Bruges, of Antwerp and Amsterdam. The gallery sits in a city built by lumber and railway barons not even two hundred years ago. Back then, we knew some of those men; but right now we are watching a woman with brown glossy skin. She carries a canvas bag slung over one shoulder.

Our woman stands waiting to see the Dutch and stares at a muscled security guard: his skin is brown, just like hers. And together he and our woman are the only brown people at the gallery, at least down in the area where one finds the Dutch. The security guard takes our woman's ticket. He folds and detaches a stub, hands it back, and when he does so, the security guard asks our woman for her canvas shoulder bag. He gives the bag a quick pat, and she's in.

We follow at a safe distance. We often attend art galleries, auction halls, estate sales and many other such places. So many currents of emotion, embalmed inside the objects people buy, sell, inherit. So many vibrations: settlement, dispossession, affluence, nostalgia. Right now we are tapping into the energy of our woman and her canvas bag as she walks, step by step, to visit the Dutch Masters.

Everywhere men and women line up behind string stretched to demarcate no-go zones around the art. Don't touch! One hundred and twenty-eight paintings from the Rijksmuseum in Amsterdam. Vermeer, Hals, Rembrandt. Everywhere there are the faces, immortal in oil, framed and brought again to life by the act of viewing. Each painting emanates the energy of the long-ago touch of its maker. The more intent the gaze, the closer the air in the gallery seems to settle, on paintings and on spectators. We crane our necks to peer at signage below the paintings. Closer, closer. There is our woman, viewing the viewed.

Someone coughs. Our woman flinches, then smiles. She does this on reflex whenever anyone coughs. Self-conscious, she catches the eye of another woman, tall and willowy, in a silk one-piece jumpsuit, who smiles, lifting a strand of long blonde hair away from her forehead. So now we are watching two women: our woman and the tall woman who looks over the top of her rimless glasses and smiles. *Do you think they've got a place for sales in here?*

Both women laugh and head to the gallery gift shop. Everywhere there is merchandise and posters, all the Dutch, all rolled up. We nod to the tall willowy woman. Her name is Sally. Years ago she taught fine art to suburban high-school students. She doesn't see us at all. We're used to that, and we smile as Sally disappears behind stacks of art books.

Inside the shop, a woman in a striped dress rests the weight of her arm against a massive stack of posters. These lie flat on a counter, and beside the posters are plastic bags emblazoned with a reproduction of Vermeer's *Milkmaid*. The woman at the counter adjusts her name tag: it reads *Martha*. Martha's thick fingers, dextrous from years of working her family's valley egg farm, snap a red rubber band around posters, one by one, and plop them into plastic bags emblazoned with the gallery logo. Martha smiles when she sees the look of interest on our woman's face. Martha keeps at her work: lift, roll, snap, plop.

"Oh, I don't think that painting is actually in the exhibit, is it?" asks our woman as she reaches for a *Milkmaid* poster. Martha, smiling, shrugs and drops another poster into a plastic bag. Our woman studies the beads of sweat on Martha's upper lip. Our woman fingers the edge of one *Milkmaid* poster. Martha pauses in her poster-rolling work and looks at our woman, who smiles in return. From the back of the gift shop, holding a heavy art book, Sally emerges.

So now we are watching these three women: Martha and her posters—lift, snap, plop; Sally, tall and willowy with her friendly smile; and our woman with her shoulder bag, which is open. Inside, we can see the edge of something. Sally sees it too, and asks our woman, "Oh, are you a student?" Our woman, startled, her hand automatically covering the paper sticking out from her shoulder bag, says, "Oh, just interested in the Dutch," and moves to the side, suddenly deeply interested in a box of cards: Vermeer's *The Love Letter*, reproduced fifteen times per box. We look at the small gift shop space, stacked with art posters and stuffed with key chains, ceramic and plastic dishes and canvas book bags. All embossed with the likeness of the paintings: Willem Claesz Heda's and Aelbert Cuyp's intricate still-life compositions.

Our woman, her brown face smooth as butter, fingers the shoulder strap of her canvas bag and studies a copy of the gallery's press release, "Celebrating the 400th Anniversary of the Dutch Landing in North America." Around her, people cram into the selling-space. They touch and buy copies of paintings, shiny reproductions affixed to surfaces, all coexisting with 'the real things' far away inside the Dutch Masters exhibit. The real and the reproduced, subjects and objects, vibrate their own wavelengths of energy. We smile at the posters. No one notices us. Yet here we are, adding to the hum of the place. Everyone feels it. No one says it.

At the cashier's desk, people stand in line, holding on to coffee mugs, books, ashtrays, T-shirts and scarves. Mouths open and eyes glazed. A voice from the back of the shop calls out, "Martha, maybe get the cash?" and Martha, without missing a beat, puts down her posters and starts ringing in merchandise. There are so many people in line, Martha doesn't see our woman, back at the counter with the posters, fingering *The Milkmaid*. Quick, our woman slips from her shoulder bag an old poster: *Man with Golden Helmet*, creased at the corners. Portrait of a soldier, his face weather-beaten from many campaigns. On his head, a large ornate gold helmet. Our woman tucks him in with the other posters. She's brought him here to join his brethren.

Our woman stands in line at the cash register. She is now communicating soundlessly — waves of jittery emotion — pulsing outward. Our woman approaches Martha at the cashier. Martha asks, "Is that everything?" Our woman nods, hands over money for her box of cards.

Martha wants to also ask, "You doing okay?" because something about the jittery energy emanating from our woman speaks soundlessly to Martha's egg-farming soul; but Martha, with one quick look at the people standing in line behind our woman, presses her lips together and keeps working the till. She works fast and forgets to give our woman a plastic bag for the Vermeer cards. Our woman doesn't mind. She wants to flee from the confines of the Dutch and the gift shop. She is almost out the shop and into the foyer of the gallery, her box of Vermeer cards in one hand, canvas bag over her shoulder, when, from the poster counter, Sally, blonde hair tucked behind her ear, art book purchased, tilts her head and in a few steps, tugs at the yellowed creased poster of *Man with Golden Helmet*.

Our woman's eyes widen. She frowns, shaking her head. Tiny movements, side to side. Sally, though, curious, pulls the old poster from its resting-hiding place. Sally says, "Oh, *Man with Golden Helmet*. Did you leave it behind here?" her voice rising louder than she intended. Startled out of their buying-things impulse, everyone in the gift shop turns as if one body and stares first at Sally and then at the yellowed poster of *Man With Golden Helmet*, its creased corners held in Sally's long fingers.

At the cash register, a man in a sports cap leans toward Martha. With one hand he points back to the gift shop entrance, to our woman hovering, and says, "Did she just steal something from inside here?" Sally, bless her, pipes up, "No, no, I think she just forgot something."

The man in the sports cap grins and turns to his wife, who is about to buy four T-shirts to give to their grandchildren.

Martha opens and closes her mouth, swallows, and before she can speak, our woman steps back inside the shop, grabs a plastic art gallery bag, and drops in Vermeer's *Milkmaid* cards and the receipt. Our woman takes her poster of *Man with Golden Helmet* from Sally's outstretched hands. Our woman's cheeks flush red. We can almost feel the rush of blood under her brown skin.

In the foyer of the gallery, our woman stands still, closes her eyes, and takes a deep breath. Her fingers grasp two bags, plastic and canvas. We watch the security guard watching our woman. She walks to the side exit by the marble steps and sits down. We follow close behind. We know these steps well. Long ago, we trod upwards to the courthouse for the trial of a man accused of killing a British officer; but that is another story for another time, and today we are watching our woman as she re-rolls her poster, clutching it to her chest. Soon, *Man with Golden Helmet* is back in our woman's canvas bag.

At the foot of those marble steps, we stand absorbed in the sounds of voices that we know no one but our woman can hear: mother, aunties, cousins, old family friends. All the timbres of accusation and scolding and disbelief reverberate inside her head: *you sure are your father's daughter, wasting time on something like that. What's wrong with you?*

These voices, like shadows, keep us company as our woman walks down to the train station. She boards an eastbound Skytrain to the town of towns, clutching her two bags. In her art gallery bag, emblazoned with *The Dutch Are Here*, her lone box of Vermeer *Love Letter* cards. In her canvas bag, that yellowed poster of *Man with Golden Helmet*, creased corners as tired as his face.

On the Skytrain, we sit in the seat just behind our woman. We stare into the back of her head. We see what no one else on the train can even guess. Our woman is time travelling! We understand perfectly, as would anyone travelling eastward on the Skytrain, following the river from city to suburbs and then to the town of towns.

We've been in communion with this town for years — we've sat in pews in a dozen churches; we've watched folks shopping in two department stores; we've watched their children buying things in malls. We've paused to admire many a garden, intent on walking the side streets and alleyways of the town. Cats, dogs, rats, skunks—small animals adept at slinking away from us—roam from water's edge down at the parkade, and then cross-town, past houses. Overhead, gulls, bald eagles, blue herons, cormorants, the occasional barn owl, lost and wandering. By evening, a handful of bats swoop against the walls of condominium towers that range against the river, down by the deserted docks. To walk from water's edge to uptown would take maybe thirty minutes, provided your legs were strong.

We are much faster, though, and in the blink of an eye we float and rise high above the river to a green hill where once a prison watched with us, the eastern approach to the city. On the hill above the prison is one of our favourite resting places, the cemetery.

Here, crows hop over graves. One crow, having taken his rest at the edge of a stone marker, flies out into oncoming traffic, where his kamikaze dive meets the windshield of an SUV. The crow drops onto pavement, spasmodic, wings bent out of shape. Silent crow, stilled. Cars slow to avoid the body. Against all odds, not seen by anyone, the crow rises again, flaps its wings into the sky above the town of towns and we fly with him.

In a flash we see the end of a world war whose gaping maw will claim the lives of many young men in the town where plaques and monuments will stand to attention. We fly from cemetery to another hill, where bulldozers churn the earth of a potter's field where Indian, Chinese, Japanese immigrants lie. And with them the bodies of First Nations, those who come before all others.

On top of this sacred/desecrated land, a secondary school will be built. From these halls, students will graduate, marry, have children, get jobs, lose jobs, divorce, remarry. No one speaks the word *asbestos*, substance as messenger, lining the walls of classrooms. No one speaks of the bones underneath the foundation of the school. The dead are not named, and if they speak, it is a ventriloquism through the upright bodies of students who roam the school. The years press forward at a rate unimaginable to previous generations, when time transmits in text talk, thumb actions that might also be scrolling backwards—see, there is our woman, in the secondary school in the town of towns.

Her teacher, Mr Struthers. Behind his stooping shoulders, students are known to call him Mr Szzz. When he speaks, with a slight stutter, several girls in the back row roll their eyes. Not our woman. Instead she looks down at her notebook, waiting for Mr Struthers' voice to resume its cadence, in whose timbre resides a vestige of his great-grandfather, a remittance man.

Mr Struthers wears a fringe of hair encircling his bald dome. He tells his Art History II class a story about the lost paintings of Rembrandt. Our woman will sit up straighter in her chair and lean in, thinking of the poster in her house, framed and propped on a shelf above the piano: dark background foregrounding a soldier, his face worn by care and campaigns of war. Furrowed brow, grey moustache, he wears a golden helmet and the armour of a centurion. He does not smile. Once upon a time, daydreams our woman, her face turned away from Mr Struthers, her eyes looking out the window to the street.

Once upon a time, there lived a man born in Bombay/Mumbai. He bought a poster reproduction of a painting by a Dutch Master, *Man with Golden Helmet*. When the time comes for voyaging to the

New World, the poster, tucked into a blue trunk, sails the ocean. In a year, the man will send for his bride. She'll bring their daughter and they'll move to Montreal, where another daughter will be born. The man and his family pack their belongings in cardboard boxes and drive across Canada. The blue trunk travels with them. Eventually, family, boxes, trunk, end up in a rented manse, the home-house in the town of towns. Down in the basement goes the blue trunk. Years later, the blue trunk will be opened, the poster unrolled and framed, set down in the piano room.

"Okay, class, remember: next week, your presentations." Mr Struthers's voice is a faint echo. Somebody at the back of the classroom snaps gum. The buzzer squawks over the crackling PA system. Mr Struthers turns his back to the class, and Art History 11, flared jeans brushing the halls, sojourns to Algebra 11, two outliers drifting to the track for a smoke.

Our woman will be the last to exit and by then, even Mr Struthers has fled to the staff room, his eyes never meeting anyone in the crowded halls, his gaze trained on the hallway, the merest suggestion of a shaking tremor as his hands pat the inside pocket of his tweed jacket. A week later, our woman will carry *Man with Golden Helmet* to his Art History class. Our woman will attempt a presentation about time travel, art, and the nature of the Real and the Reproduced. A few students look at our woman, their heads nodding. Most of the class, though, smirk, chew gum, whisper and giggle. Long after even the janitor has buffed the floors of the room, we are still inside, gathering vibrations, the ones that summon us from courthouse to art gallery; from cemeteries to schools to the little-used stacks of libraries or old dusty bookstores.

In one of these bookstores, a few years later, our woman will again meet Mr Struthers, who greets her with a wan smile. He stands a little apart from our woman. She pretends not to see the small square bottle tucked under his tweed jacket. A woman in a bright pink fleece tracksuit enters the bookstore. Our woman and her teacher step to the back. They sit in two overstuffed chairs, donations from one of the families that first settled the town. Our woman says, "Do you remember my father's copy of *Man with Golden Helmet*?" And her teacher says, "How could I forget?"

Our woman regales Mr Struthers with the stories from her life witnessed by *Man with Golden Helmet*: her first stolen kiss, right there in that piano room with a young man named Rory; her first scholarship rejection (there would be more), the ripped letter lying abandoned on the piano bench and that soldier, eyes downcast.

On a Saturday in November, before first snowfall, our woman's fingers pause on the piano keys. She glances up at *Man with Golden Helmet*. Is there maybe the merest ripple of an expression, as if the soldier's downturned mouth lifted—his face underneath his golden armour, not looking out at the viewer, a soldiers' soldier, home from the wars. Our woman sighs and returns to her piano practice. She does not look again at the soldier and his golden helmet. Would she have spotted us then? We moved without any noise from right beside the piano, through the window, to the winter garden.

"You were, then, more fanciful, I suppose," says Mr Struthers with the sweetest smile. Our woman raises her eyebrows and laughs.

"Well, I had been, *like*, practising arpeggios, Bach and Brahms, for *hours*. Not. For some reason that day—oh, I don't know—I swear I saw something. I told my father. He smiled at me the way you are doing right now. He said, "I read somewhere that Rembrandt painted, again and again, his own face onto every subject he ever drew."

The smile on Mr Struthers's face deepens. He doesn't interrupt our woman. He doesn't say, "No, that was me, I told you that." Mr Struthers instead reaches one trembling hand to his jacket pocket and sits deeper in the overstuffed chair. He closes his eyes.

Our woman browses books. She turns her head sideways to the crammed shelves; but we know that instead of book titles, she's seeing her father's face. He stands in the doorway to the piano room, about to turn away, already late for a meeting, but he pauses. Did he see something move in the garden? Father and daughter turn their heads to peer out the piano-room window. There is only the wind on trees, whose bare branches tap out a forlorn rhythm on lead-paned glass.

The light in the bookstore fades, and a dog barks out on the street. Our woman turns her head away from the bookshelves. Mr Struthers turns his head to the front of the bookshop. They both look in the direction we are looking to catch a glimpse of the late afternoon sunlight through the dusty windows. When we brush past Jim, the bookshop owner, he glances at our woman and Mr Struthers: his two best customers. Jim suppresses a chuckle. He knows they won't be leaving anytime soon. Our woman and Mr Struthers gossip about one of his former students, Cora-Lynn. "That girl drove me crazy with her gum chewing," says Mr Struthers, and our woman says, "Cora-Lynn was a champion."

One afternoon, Cora-Lynn from up the street visits our woman. And yes, we are again at the home-house. We sit on an orange-red velvet settee, *Man with Golden Helmet* at his place, his downcast eyes averted from the unplayed piano. Cora-Lynn works the

Sunday shift at the Dairy Queen and on her walk home carries a tray of practice treats. Our woman and Cora-Lynn eat Peanut Buster Parfaits.

Cora-Lynn rises from the velvet settee and faces *Man with Golden Helmet*. She wrinkles her nose. "I don't like it," she says between scoops of Dairy Queen ice cream.

Our woman licks the parfait and says, "But it's good, really. I mean, good job."

Cora-Lynn snorts, gesturing to the plastic spoon halfway to our woman's pink-brown lips.

"Not that," says Cora-Lynn. "This." And Cora-Lynn jabs a pudgy finger toward the painting. Then, with a sideways look, between licks of ice cream, Cora-Lynn says, "Don't get mad, but Mom asked me to ask you, and don't get all weird——"

Our woman eats her DQ treat, eyes fixed on the ice cream, when Cora-Lynn asks, "What kind of Canadian are you, anyway?"

Unseen on the velvet settee, we shift, balancing our weight, grateful that our size combined isn't a match for Cora-Lynn. We look at Cora-Lynn's sly smile, her pudgy fingers. We look at our woman. For a moment, she just keeps licking her Peanut Buster Parfait. She licks the ice cream and crunches down on the peanuts. Lick-crunch. Lick-crunch. We look at the downturned face of the man with the golden helmet, and cannot at this moment read his eyes, averted forever.

Neither of the girls says anything further. Neither hears our sighs. Cora-Lynn watches our woman and says, "Next time I'll make us a triple-chocolate sundae."

The two girls sit on that velvet settee. We are quiet as church mice. This certainly isn't the time to say something about Cora-Lynn and how Cora-Lynn will ask our woman to be maid of honour at Cora-Lynn's wedding (pink sateen floor-length dresses); about how Cora-Lynn's first daughter, born on Christmas Day, will one day — oh, how the years rush back and forth —

In the bookstore, seated next to her teacher, our woman brushes a tear off her face. Mr Struthers says nothing. His trembling hands turn the pages of a book about the river. From the stack on the floor, our woman runs her thumb against the edge of a 1979 Yellow Pages.

That summer our woman's father devises a kind of exercise room in the basement of the home-house. Our woman never tells anyone what goes on down there. Y-O-G-A. Cora-Lynn will ask our woman to spell y-o-g-a and will not, although urged to do so, approach our woman's mother, who from her kitchen kingdom in the home-house harrumphs and look askance when our woman's father, in a T-shirt and underwear, begins his descent to the basement for morning poses. When Cora-Lynn visits, she will tell our woman, "I don't know anyone else like you." Not one of our woman's friends, including Cora-Lynn, will hear the soft thump of the *Manchester Guardian* delivered through their mail slots on Friday afternoons, whispery-thin onion skin paper, brown paper wrapping stamped, surface to surface, third class.

In their neighbourhood, at that time, there are no personal computers except for the Apple IIe our woman's father will purchase and tinker with. But that is later in the decade. There are no iPods, iPads, Blackberrys, or other electronic devices. There is no Internet.

Our woman and her sister are seated at the breakfast table in the kitchen. Their mother sighs. Our woman and her sister exchange eye-rolls. Maybe yoga is something illicit, maybe even perverted. "Dad, do you do yoga, in, you know the N-U-D-E?!

And they shriek with laughter, and their mother harrumphs and gets up to wash their breakfast dishes, and their father laughs and says, "Oh, ye of little knowledge, who know so little of time's arrows." Or something like that. Our translation from Marathi, his mother tongue, is perhaps imprecise.

And then the next day, without saying anything to anyone, our woman's father lifts *Man with Golden Helmet* from the piano room shelf, and down it goes, to the basement. The old soldier's reproachful face will keep our woman's father company for years of yoga practice complemented by daily doses of green tea, flax cookies, unbleached whole-grain flour and stacks of the *Berkeley Wellness Letter*. We see our woman's father down there in the home-house basement: his compact brown body, downward dog to finishing poses. We know our woman's father will do these moves devotedly, trying to stave off, as so many do, that moment, when—we understand. Life is, after all, a kind of *negotiation*, and we are masters of the Great Barter, and we never interfere.

One day, our woman will bring home to the piano room a novel. It is *Green Darkness* by Anya Seton, in which the characters travel back in time, reincarnated from 1960s England to the 1500s. Our woman's father catches his daughter reading rather than playing the piano. He sits down on the orange-red velvet settee and they talk about time. We have joined them. We are intrigued. Our woman's father tells his daughter that time is its own dimension, the past always present. She, being young, just rolls her eyes and goes upstairs to her home-house bedroom. Her father lingers a while in the piano room. He looks up, quickly, just once, to the shelf where once sat his companion, *Man with Golden Helmet.*

On the shelf behind his cash register, the silver mahogany clock chimes eight in the evening. We watch Jim the bookshop owner. We've been watching his family for decades, from when they first arrived at this west coast place, through two world wars, the Great Depression, through boom and bust years, always somehow hanging on. Jim shuts his cash register, counts his meagre earnings, locks the front door, flips the open sign to closed, and wanders to the back of the shop. He returns with three wine glasses and a bottle of red. Mr Struthers, with a courtly flourish, finally takes out from under his tweed jacket his small square bottle and says, "No red for me there, young Jim." Mr Struthers pours a thumb's length of Scotch into his glass, which he raises, saying, "This town!" Jim and our woman laugh and raise their wine glasses.

Closing time anywhere is always a great time: we listen to Mr Struthers expounding his theory of Rembrandt as a time traveller interested in the evocation of atmosphere by use of oils to evoke light and time of day. Our woman can't bear to tell him she's heard his theory before, in Art History II. She nods her head, thinking again of the secondary school and the parking lot fronting Eighth Street. The lot, crescent shaped and adjacent to a plaza, curves into a driveway bordered by huge rhododendron, sentinels fitted into raised stone.

Late August and our woman is with a young man, Rory. His family built the first grocery store down by the river, on land bought at a 'reasonable price' from a group of Chinese rail workers, themselves squatters on the ancient territory of the Qayqayt Nation.

Rory and our woman are preparing to compete for CBC's *Reach for the Top* program. Rory's voice grates over-loud when he speaks. Rory doesn't mean to be so loud. Somehow his being loud happens when he's nervous. Rory says, "*Man with Golden Helmet*, it's Rembrandt, you know." He says the name with a flourish, the initial R sound rattles from his chiselled lips into the dry summer air. Rory, who insists on his Scottish heritage, is in fact ten percent Scottish and ninety percent everything else, his origin story so complex we will have to keep it close until our next meeting.

In the bookstore, the teacher says, "I remember you and Rory!" At this our woman shoots a look at Mr Struthers, who permits himself a small laugh that he makes into a small cough. "Hmm. What I meant was good old *Reach for the Top!* Good old CBC!"

In the darkened bookshop, Jim, our woman, and Mr Struthers talk about the good old CBC ("a shade of its former self"); they talk about Rembrandt and his last lost painting.

When our woman asks, "Do you think there's an outside chance that *Man with Golden Helmet* is actually a lost Rembrandt painting?" Mr Struthers shakes his head and says, "Oh, that would be a very long shot," and then they speak of other things. Two years later she will see him again, walking down Columbia Street. He'll be dead in a week. And the bookshop owner, Jim, from that old settler family. No one now knows his whereabouts, but some say Jim was last seen driving a '69 Ford truck loaded in back with boxes of books, on a rip-rap road upcountry, way past the Pitt River.

It cannot be that the poster of *Man with Golden Helmet* sits still in that basement, but we have made it so. What quality of air now circulates within the space created by beams and boards? We cannot answer. In the far corner, by a makeshift shower stall and on a mat, dressed in cotton underwear, as if a mere dhoti of loincloth, a fine-boned man bends into his asana poses. His companion is solemn with immobility, knowing and un/knowing the calamities that will occur during this companionship: a murder on the next street; a rape in the park across from that street. Several wars overseas. The denial of the building of a high school over land that may or may not contain the bones of First Nations and Chinese and East Indian and ne'er-do-wells. *Man with Golden Helmet* hears rumours, gossip, anecdotes: that the school rises upon a pauper's cemetery, a potter's field. It is the future forward and it is the past, back into the 1940s. A school needs to be built.

We see a man small in stature, balding and brown-skinned. Of course we know his birthdate: January 28, 1937. And his end-date: April 19, 2002, morning, just past 8:15 a.m., alone in the hospital in the town of towns, his daughters away from him and his wife also. They will soon join his body. They will be called. It is always happening, the way moments become the years.

The poster stays on by the makeshift shower stand. Dust covered, downcast as ever. In the days following her father's death, our woman wanders down to the basement. She finds the old soldier propped on a ledge — cedar planks affixed to the unfinished concrete wall of the house. She strokes a finger across the glass surface of the poster, framed in oak, so cobwebbed her fingers trail a furrowed track. When she brushes the surface, gold shows through. She lifts the poster in its oak frame. And then it happens. The thing falls apart. There is no proper backing.

Her father, busy school trustee, ordained minister visiting the sick, organizing protests against wage cutbacks, jammed his print copy of the Dutch Master into a rummage-sale oak frame: no time for craftsmanship, little concern for home-handiness, no veneration for the object. He'd just shoved it in, in honour of what he saw: a soldier's face, battle ready, in uniform, but tired. A subject averted from his maker, an ocean voyager, a yoga companion for a makeshift exercise area in a decrepit basement. The poster creased and yellowed. Our woman laughs and says out loud, "Dad!" We are the only ones to hear the sound in that dank basement in the home-house in the towns of towns. Our woman shakes her head, sets the ill-framed object back on its dusty ledge and walks away.

Four years after the death of our woman's father, her mother sells the home-house, and after neglect and procrastination, the basement is cleared. A repository of thirty years in one place: clothes, books, unrepaired appliances, boxes, hundreds of magazines—the *Economist*, the *New Internationalist (old version)*, *Time*, *Newsweek*, the *Christian Century*, the *Catholic Daily Worker*, the *Times Literary Supplement*, stacks of white, onion-skin thin *Manchester Guardian*, *National Geographic* from 1940 to the new century, tossed, thrown out and junked. People come and go. *Man with Golden Helmet* watches from his perch, leaning against an unfinished basement wall. One day, just before the sale, we will go down to the empty basement—and he will be gone.

December 30, 2013. As found by us after midnight, a letter left on an old oak desk:

Dear Dad,

I write this in my office down by the Fraser River. The home-house now sold to a woman named Marjorie. She keeps up with Mom, and from time to time invites us to visit 820 Dublin Street: the home-house. I never go back.

To my left—a view of the river. And on my mahogany desk, that yellowed poster copy of Man with Golden Helmet: *he is propped against the office wall, stained print attached to cardboard with three pressed balls of green painter's tape, the cardboard hoarded from a condo recycling bin. Miss you forever.*

Man with Golden Helmet

You will probably know, as we've known for years: *Man with Golden Helmet* is not really a Rembrandt at all. *The New York Times* and *Time Magazine*, in 1985, published articles about its "defrocking from the canon"—an essayist, one Otto Friedrich, writes an elegy to a copy of the painting as hung in his father's living room. Still later, in the age of the Internet, fathomless territory where watchers like us are relegated to ever distant atmospheres—where, should you wish to sense us, you'll need to learn to look over your shoulder—a blog article appears on the website *Caffeinated Joe.* The writer recalls seeing a copy of *Man with Golden Helmet* down in not only his parents' basement but his aunt's as well.

We should mention that the art gallery is majestic in its plans for a new location, and our woman, living in the city, rarely visits the town of towns, where a new secondary school emerges. As always, we are busy, watching at airports, ferry terminals, borders and other ports of entry: everywhere still that ash-laden, whispering wind, which on grey afternoons, eastward along the Skytrain line by the river, will find us back at the cemetery on the hill with the crows.

Shall we walk? Here. Here is the grave of a man deceased, who as a boy once ran the beaches of Mumbai, at Juhu. That man and his poster. What remains with us now are two crows who sit at the edge of a stone marker where once our kamikaze crow perched and where once the man's two daughters visited at month's end. Their absence is noted by the crows, in whose brains reside no hints of nostalgia, nor of hymns, nor of any stored image. We are the only ones to see the two women who bend toward stone, speaking words to the words they find there engraved: "Fare Forward Voyagers!"

And here we are, asking you to picture our soldier, *Man with Golden Helmet*, a representation of a representation once thought to be by a Master, dislodged from that authorship. His careworn face is alive in poster-copy, churned out by the thousands, perhaps millions. And in tiny print at the bottom: "1129, copyright 1975, Haddad's Fine Arts, Inc, California." Look with us, bend down right now. See? Now, look up to the river. Where flies the crow, there is a green hill far away.

Dear *Man with Golden Helmet*,

We haven't seen you in some time, and we can't remember where you are …

Renée Sarojini Saklikar

Pulp Literature: 'Man with Golden Helmet' is part ghost story, part mystery, part memoir. How did it come to be?

Renée Sarojini Saklikar: I began writing 'Man with Golden Helmet' many years ago in response to a writing prompt given to students in a SFU writing class. We were looking at ways to access memory and the imagination, particularly when writing memoir. So often, students will say, "But I just can't remember enough detail to fill in my narrative." One tip is to use the imagination to get closer to a particular memory.

I gave my students a set of prompts that riffed on the poem 'Those Winter Sundays' by Robert Hayden ("Sundays, too, my father got up early"). I asked students to think about images/sounds/actions related to one of their parents and a day of the week.

For example, I remember my mother, a South Asian immigrant, baking bread on Saturdays because that's what she learned from the women of St John's, Newfoundland, when we first came to Canada.

Once we situated our scene with a family member and a day of the week, I invited students to then layer in geography and place.

I always like to do the writing prompts with students, and that day, instead of following the thread of memory with my mother baking bread, I followed a particular image of the landscape and geography of New Westminster, where eventually—from India to Newfoundland, to Quebec, and then across the prairies—we came to live.

Place, location, time, dates, names: these are obsessions that come up repeatedly in my writing. And so too, are ghosts. I've always loved ghost stories!

PL: At *Pulp,* we publish diverse genres and authors writing cross-genre, and 'Man with Golden Helmet' is such a wonderful example of that multiplicity. Similarly, much of your work appears in other creative forms, such as visual and performance art and opera. Are there any other artistic forms or genres you would like to explore?

RSS: I'd love to combine oral/aural experiences of narrative, such as podcasts and videos, with the process of writing. For example, I've been playing around with using my iPhone to document when I'm shredding paper: the sound of the paper being shredded. Or the sound my Sharpie pen makes as it scratches its way across my notebook. I'm fascinated by language as material, the way a potter might use clay. The way the poet/artist Chris Turnbull uses language in outdoor art installations.

There's a beautiful series she's done with one of my poems, and you can see photos of that on my website, the-canadaproject.wordpress.com/what-is-thecanadaproject/thot-j-bap-collaboration-with-chris-turnbull/

Chris and I have been thinking about ways we can go deeper with collaborating: mixing poetry and video. When I reflect on this, I realize that visual aspects of language, the way language works on a page, is really important to me: all of my books include artwork and photographs and text in concrete arrangements, in addition to 'regular storytelling'.

PL: Continuing with the idea of artistic hybridity, in *Listening to the Bees*, co-authored with scientist Mark L Winston, we discover poetry, essays, and photographs that draw on the scientific, poetic, personal, and communal. Could you speak to the importance of collaboration and communication across disciplines?   .

RSS: A wonderful question. Looking back on my body of work (I can't believe how I have one now!), I always feel like I'm just a beginner, which, I'm coming to realize, is a gift. So, looking at my books, my chapbooks, the opera made out of my first book, the musical adaptation of my bee poems, the work with Chris Turnbull, yes, I think I'm drawn to different artistic disciplines and learn

a great deal from musicians, composers, dancers, visual artists. I'm fascinated with the process of how they make art, how long it takes to get something *just right*, the amount of labour involved, the number of drafts, rehearsals… Somehow that gives me sustenance as I'm a slow writer, slower reader, and we live in such a fast-paced, distracted world. I'm really drawn to artists and creators who take the time to do deep. Last night, for instance, I clicked on *The New York Times* ('doom scrolling'! I admit it) and the first thing I saw was this piece on the pianist Lang Lang and his long-time project with Bach: udiscovermusic.com/classical-news/lang-lang-goldberg-variations/

PL: Is there anyone with whom you would like to collaborate?

RSS: Yes! I'd love to continue working with Turning Point Ensemble director and composer Owen Underhill as well as Irish composer Jürgen Simpson (they created the opera *air india redacted* based on my first book). And as I've mentioned, Chris Turnbull and I hope to do more video/narrative work.

As well, in 2017 I was commissioned by New Works and the Vancouver Public Library to create a poetry/dance installation with acclaimed dancer Salome Nieto, and we performed this amazing piece, *Happiness,* on the ninth floor of the Vancouver Public Library, outside!

In writing and reflecting on your thoughtful questions I am reminded of the terrible toll this pandemic is taking on performing arts and artists. Gratitude and much respect to all the makers out there, all the musicians, dancers, visual artists, theatre makers, and all their gigs. Tough times. I'm so grateful that *Pulp Lit* is publishing!

PL: This year marks the thirty-fifth anniversary of the Air India

bombing that killed your aunt and uncle and has been fundamental to much of your work. How, as Canadians, do you believe we should be speaking about and addressing atrocity?

RSS: Oh, so very carefully, and with nuance and love and compassion. How to give witness to the pain of others. How to hold compassionate space for the enormity of loss resulting from mass murder: I don't have any tailor-made, easy response. How to be there for people, how to listen more… Shanti (peace). I tried to set down some of these thoughts, earlier this year, in a piece commissioned by *Chatelaine* magazine: chatelaine. com/news/iran-plane-crash-air-india/

PL: Could you tell us about *thecanadaproject,* your life-long poem chronicle, and your decision to change the name to *thecanada?project?*

RSS: *thecanadaproject* is a concept that seemed to come to me the more I delved into writing poetry and narrative: the idea that the work is the life and vice versa. As well, from the get-go, I realized I write in cycles, sagas, chronicles, series: each image, each snippet of verse, each scene in a story is honed and important. But always, with me, the singular is part of something bigger, longer. It's very rarely that I sit down and write one lonesome poem.

The writer Gary Snyder, in his book *The Real Work,* talks about this idea, as does SFU English prof Dr Stephen Collis, whose work has had an influence on my thinking about this.

In this, our pandemic, it's both poignant and kinda scary, this idea: that the project lives as I live and will end when I end…

The decision to change the name was part of a long journey in starting to come to terms with the moral urgency of the truth-telling and reconciliation process with Indigenous peoples: I grew up, as I've said, living across Canada, and my parents, like many immigrant-settlers, instilled in me an idealistic and gratitude-based feeling for all this country has given us.

That basic feeling — of gratitude for the people who built this country; for Medicare and Tommy Douglas (will we ever see the likes of him again?); and for public education and public transit and parks and green space — that is still very strong with me. Maybe now, in this pandemic, more than ever.

And at the same time, from a very early age (my parents once taught for what was then the Department of Indian Affairs in Northern Ontario and Northern Quebec), there was also in me, as a brown woman — who, as a little girl, didn't know what kind of Indian I was (I was asked that a lot, growing up: "What kind of Indian are you?") — this deep unease about what this entity, Canada, was/is.

And this unease just grew until quite recently when, as I write about on my website, I was privileged to be invited as a guest to UBC's Indian Residential School History and Dialogue Centre: irshdc.ubc.ca/. And everything just coalesced for me, and I started revisiting things I'd known. But now, because of the experience at the centre and our cultural moment with Indigenous writers and activists, something just split open for me…

I'm still processing all of it. And I realized I can't just, in all honesty, continue as if nothing has changed. I have to hold my own work accountable.

So a very small but profound step for me is this breaking up, this un/settling of my own lifelong project and its 'brand' or title, on the level of my most fundamental tool as a working writer, language. Thus *thecanada?project?*

PL: On your blog, you talk about 2019 as being your 'testing year' in which you relearned *to persist*. How did the lessons of 2019 prepare you to persist in 2020?

RSS: I'm still processing that! The year 2019 was tough; but man, 2020? Holy moly. And 'it ain't over yet'. Maybe you will ask me this in December? I don't want to jinx anything. We all need all the grace and luck we can get. One thing about this idea, persistence: I see it around me every day. Starting with my husband, who never gives up. Despite many obstacles, he just keeps on going. And my family. We've known unimaginable tragedy, yet still, to keep going … that's the thing, right? I've tried to think of this pandemic, for all its tragedy and *bad*, as a gift to take the time to get deeper into writing.

PL: As a poet laureate, writing instructor, and contest judge (including for *Pulp*'s Magpie Awards), what is your greatest wish for emerging poets?

RSS: Love yourself. Loving yourself will help you with the work. Loving yourself will open you to the idea of creating and building and sustaining a writing practice. Something you do every day, no matter what. Building a practice, you create a body of work. So much then starts to happen. Love yourself. Do the work. Build the practice.

PL: In this digital age, with overflowing news feeds and constant connectivity, what helps you find a stillpoint?

RSS: Walks outside in the green spaces we are so blessed to have around us. Being with loved ones. Doing yoga. Prayer.

PL: Thank you for making the time to speak with us. Before we go, could you tell us a little about what you are working on now?

RSS: Thank you for these lovely, thoughtful questions. I'm working on three things. A new book project for which I got my first Canada Council grant! A self-help book about becoming. And an epic, over ten years in the making, called *THOT J BAP, The Heart of This Journey Bears All Patterns,* which I hope will soon be with a publisher … Stay tuned.

THE EXTRA: FRANKIE RAY, THE SLEUTH WITH THE PLATINUM HAIR

Mel Anastasiou

Mel Anastasiou writes the Fairmount Manor Mysteries, starring Mrs Stella Ryman; the Hertfordshire Pub Mysteries, starring Spencer Stevens; and the Monument Studios Mysteries, starring Frankie Ray and Connie Mooney. She teaches the 'Writing Success' segment of Pulp Literature Press's writing school, Quit the Day Job, and she wrote the steampunk-themed The Writer's Boon Companion: Thirty Days Towards an Extraordinary Volume *and* The Writer's Friend and Confidante.

POLICEMAN
City of Los Angeles
2563

The Extra: A Monument Studios Mystery

Previously . . .

Hollywood, April 1934. On the movie set, Frankie Ray loses track of her friend Connie, wins a walk-on role in a Monument Studios production, and rescues reluctant prostitute Billie Starr from a high-end brothel. But back at Paradise Gardens, she and Billie discover the corpse of movie star Gilbert Howard on Frankie's living-room sofa. When the police accuse Frankie of Howard's murder, the young community of extras unites to help her escape with the boy next door, the enigmatic Eugene Ellery. Eugene is a policeman himself, or so he says, but Frankie is beginning to doubt whether Eugene has her best interests in mind.

Chapter One

Eugene turned away from the window and led Frankie into his unlit bedroom. He switched on the bedside lamp, twin to the one with the iron base and ruffled shade next to her bed in Villa 7B. Like her own and Connie's bedroom next door,

Eugene's bedroom was equipped with a built-in closet and twin beds. His bedroom felt a bit roomier than theirs, for he had apparently taken the second bed to bits. The mattress and frame stood against the wall, covering the window that opened, like onto the back lawn he shared with 7A.

"You're a policeman, Eugene." Frankie clenched her fists and moderated her tone. She felt as if she were back in front of the camera, acting brave and calm. "As this is a murder case, what will happen now?"

"There will be a door-to-door search. Despite the best efforts of the Queen's kids to cover your absence, the police will have noticed by now that you are missing. And since we're the first door the police will knock on, we'll have to move quickly."

Move where? Did you think of that before you convinced me to run away? Frankie scowled. She was tired of acting brave when really she was angry. She couldn't say another word lest she raise her voice in fury at Ellery and give herself away to the police outside. She had never realized that being accused of murder would make her so angry she'd want to kill somebody.

Or was this burning emotion really anger? Very hot and very cold materials were said to feel the same. Perhaps *in extremis*, anger and fear were also indistinguishable. With an effort she kept her peace and scanned Eugene's bedroom for a hiding place.

She saw only two alternatives: under the bed or in the clothes closet built into the wall. There was nothing else in the room large enough to conceal her. She shook her head and headed for the bedroom door.

Eugene took her by the arm. "You must not leave. You'll be arrested."

Frankie could keep quiet no longer, and she found her tongue, or her tongue found her. "You're a policeman. Why don't *you* arrest me?"

Eugene released her arm. They stared at one another. Eugene lowered his eyes.

"Frankie, I watched how you treated Gilbert Howard—with honour. I know you didn't kill him. I'll stand by you as long as you need me."

Frankie swallowed. Something tied up tight inside her loosened a little. She thanked him, but she still felt like a mouse attempting to conceal itself inside an open orange crate.

Eugene said, "Hide in my closet."

Frankie followed his gaze from the tidy row of clothing on hangers to several pairs of shoes lined up on the floor. The police would enter his bedroom and find her in seconds. She imagined the satisfaction in their voices: *Now we've got you.*

She said, "That closet is the second place they'll look, right after they check underneath your bed. I'm going to have to run out the back and keep to the shadows. I've got my car out on Sunset, and I'll take my chances that the city cops don't have my description yet."

"You won't get ten feet from my door." With a clatter he shoved the clothing in his closet to either end of the rod, leaving an open space in the middle. There followed a businesslike click of wood on wood as he removed a secret door at the back of the closet. This door was cut along the bevels of the original construction, and could be replaced without any obvious seam. Inside, the space was dark.

Eugene said, "Amazing, isn't it? It might have been made expressly for hiding innocent women suspected of murder."

You won't get ten feet from my door, Eugene had said. It almost sounded like a threat. The choice was clear: stick with Eugene and his closet, or take a chance on a dash for the Model A. Which meant the choice was between a hiding place that looked like a trap but probably wasn't, or a race for what seemed like it might be freedom but would very likely result in capture. Neither of these alternatives appealed. What Frankie most wanted was to throw herself down on Eugene's chenille-covered bed and sob with fatigue and distress.

Instead she climbed in among Eugene's suit jackets, trousers and shirts, all smelling, like their owner, of Burma-Shave. Once inside his closet, she peered through the opening in the false back of the cupboard. As she had suspected, there was just about enough space inside to hide her.

"I left my money under the sofa where Gilbert Howard is sitting—"

"I'll search for it tomorrow morning. I'll bring it to you. I promise."

"Thank you, Eugene. You are a faithful fellow."

"That I am," he replied. "Faithful until death. And past it, I might add."

Somebody knocked at the front door.

Frankie dived into the closet. With a wiggling motion, she made her way through the hole to land in the little cubby at the back. She'd expected the floor to be gritty and hard, and she was not disappointed.

She heard the click of wood on wood, and then she was alone in the small unlit space.

At a second click, she started, but it was Eugene again. "You'd better take this with you." An object clattered onto the floor near her feet. "And be quiet—the wall you're leaning against adjoins the living room in 7B. Blanche Carver is still in there with any policemen who aren't searching Paradise Gardens."

"All right," she breathed. He slipped the false back of the closet into place.

In the dark, Frankie wrapped her arms around her legs and rested her chin on her knees. Her back was to her own Villa 7B's living room, where Gilbert Howard's body sat upright on her couch. The wall in front of her was shared with Eugene's living room. She got to her knees, leaned forward, and pressed her ear to the wall. Among the buzz of voices, two sounded deeper than Eugene's—the police, of course—but she couldn't make out any words.

She remembered that Eugene had thrown something that clattered—something made of metal, perhaps—into the little space with her. She felt around the floor with both hands and discovered a small heap of cloth—no, of clothing. She could feel seams and buttons, which she tucked out of the way to bunch the clothing beneath her. The fabric made a welcome bit of cushion for her backside.

Were the police gone?

No. Men exchanged mumbled words on the other side of the wall. Nearby, a door cracked open.

Eugene said, "In here, fellows. Please, look where you like. I wouldn't want to harbour a murderess under my bed."

In her hiding place, Frankie scowled at the epithet.

A male voice called Eugene *mister* and thanked him. A second added, "Please step out of our way."

That wiped her scowl away. She had never before been hunted by the police, but she was astounded to recognize the feeling all the same. It was very much like playing sardines at parties, this tension of waiting to be found. Was this how an animal felt when it was prey? This lit-up, rapid-pulse sense of expectation? In her mind's eye she saw the neon ceiling in the Dominion Theatre: the shining robes of the Goddess, the sharp eye of the Hunter, and the stags leaping away from the arc of his bow. How could the Hunter miss?

The Hunter wouldn't miss. And neither would the police, she thought, as one of them let out a throaty noise. She guessed that this was not a policeman who got down on hands and knees to look under beds too often. Gilbert Howard had been an important movie star, and the station would have sent their top men to look into his murder. Top men got soft from working at their desks. But top men were smart — smart enough, perhaps, to spot a false back in a cupboard.

Frankie strained to hear the click of the cupboard door opening, holding her breath as if it were a mouthful of water she mustn't swallow or spill. When the sound didn't come, she realized that Eugene was clever enough to have left the closet door open on purpose, to lend an air of innocence to the room — but she heard his clothes being moved aside, the hangers clicking on the rod.

She wrapped her hands around her middle. If Eugene Ellery had killed Gilbert Howard, now would be the moment for him to lean forward with a keen eye and tap the back wall of the cupboard. *What's in here, fellows? Shall we have a look?* And they'd find her in the dark.

Her heart beat faster and she felt dizzy. When they found her, what would they say? Something like, *The jig is up, sister.*

What would she answer? She would need to be hard like Barbara Stanwyck and sharp like Marietta Valdes. She mouthed the words, *Let go of me, copper. I can walk by myself.*

It was warm in the cupboard, but the shivers took her, and she fumbled in the cloth around her to see whether there might be a sweater. Her fingertips brushed a hard object on the floor. This must be the object that Eugene had tossed inside with her before shutting the door to her hiding place.

She had found the gun.

Silently she picked up the weapon and cradled it in her hands. It might be Eugene Ellery's gun — he was a policeman, and he would have a gun, wouldn't he? But she knew it wasn't Eugene's, even before she rubbed along the grip of the gun and caught the tip of her thumbnail on the lines of the crown etched there. This was the gun that had first appeared at the audition — the gun with which Gilbert Howard had shot Leo Samson in the shoulder.

It was the gun that Connie had taken from the audition in Vancouver and stowed in the Model A's glove box. King Samson had taken it back, and Marietta Valdes had taken it from him in turn before she flung it over the side of the cliff. Leo had retrieved this gun and given it to his father, who had forgotten it in Frankie's car. Frankie had lost it again in the bushes behind Paradise Gardens. There she'd believed it safely concealed.

Now, in this little room, she was learning that there was no such thing as safe concealment. Somebody had found the gun in the bushes. Somebody had shot Gilbert Howard with it. Now, Eugene had tossed it in with her. Had Eugene fired it? Had he killed Gilbert Howard? But Eugene appeared sincerely respectful of the dead actor. And furthermore, if Eugene was the killer, then why would he help her?

Outside her hiding place, Eugene's bedroom grew quiet. Perhaps the police had already left. Was the room too quiet? Maybe they were waiting for her. She pictured policemen poised on each side of Eugene's bedroom door, ready to spring upon her.

She hefted the gun from one hand to the other. She might have to fire it. Not *at* somebody, though. She'd fire it down into the floor. Better still, she'd shoot bullets up through the ceiling and make her escape in a snow of falling plaster.

She rolled onto her side and, at the sound of a tiny click from inside her pocket, and only just saved herself from crushing the men's sunglasses and breaking the bottle of peroxide Billie had stolen for her from the drugstore.

She mouthed, *I'm no murderer, your honour. I'm a victim of society.* Indeed, she was as much a victim of society as Billie Starr.

Footsteps tapped the bedroom floor. She heard the snick of wood against wood. She shrank back against the cupboard wall and held up the gun.

Eugene hissed, "All right?"

She lowered the gun and managed to open her dry mouth. "Abso-tively."

"Don't move, Frankie. There are police all over Paradise Gardens. Let's keep the status quo, shall we?"

"Posi-lutely. Eugene, where did you get this gun?"

"Now, that was a lucky thing," Eugene said.

"Was it?" she asked.

"I spotted it in the grass outside your back door at Villa 7B. I'm certainly glad I found it before the local cops did. Sleep as well as you can." The door to the opening clicked shut.

In the darkness, Frankie touched the soft articles of clothing she'd found. A woman must have left them behind in this space at some time in the past. What woman? An actress, of course, like Frankie. A former resident of Villa 7A. Had she left the clothes hidden here when she gave up her dreams and went home a failure? Or was it for a joyful reason? Had the woman who lived here discarded these, her old clothes, when she became a success in the movies? At the very least, Frankie hoped it was not a story like Billie's.

Nor a story like Frankie's own.

How had she come to this point? In films, a series of violent energies united to make murder. But these last hours seemed thick with blind, random events that flashed like lightning, snapped themselves whip-like around her, and dragged her into the centre of the storm that had killed Gilbert Howard. Worse, her involvement might so easily have been avoided if she'd stayed home in Vancouver. But if she hadn't accompanied Connie to Hollywood, perhaps it would have been Connie hiding in Eugene's closet, accused of murder.

What if Frankie herself had somehow *set off* the concatenation of circumstances that resulted in poor Gilbert Howard sitting up dead on her sofa next door? Had her arrival in Hollywood somehow set events in motion, strained tempers, and exacerbated great-minded jealousies and ambitions so that somebody killed him? She shook her head. Impossible. A substitute schoolteacher from Vancouver was a distant outsider in Hollywood's power circles. Frankie couldn't affect the fate of a fly.

The air in the cubby was heavy but not stifling, so there had to be an opening somewhere. Moving noiselessly, she plumped up the clothing—there was a slip, judging from the lace and satin, and a blouse with inconveniently large buttons. She pulled a coat's arms tighter around her to feel a little less alone. She wished Connie were here. She recognized this as an ungenerous thought—the hiding place was too small for two, and she didn't want her friend to be hunted by the law—but still she wished Connie were here. She tried to worry about her, but the cold truth was that Connie wasn't in a dark nook with the police searching for her as a murderess. She was certainly somewhere better than this. In imagination, Frankie heard Connie ask in radio announcer tones, *What do you want in a hiding place, Frankie?*

I want a pillow that smells as fresh as summer rain . . .

. . . and a gun.

Frankie wondered whether a police photographer had already come, and if Gilbert Howard's body was gone by now. She remembered his white hand and the way his fingers had curled around the orange. The hairs on his fingers, black against his skin. She sat up straight. His white hand looked the same as the hand of the body buried under the lawn outside Villas 7A and B. Not as dirty, perhaps, but certainly the same hand.

That meant there was only one dead man in Paradise Gardens, and that man was Gilbert Howard. Somebody had first of all buried him out back of Villa A where she had watched Eugene uncover his dead hand. Then somebody had finished digging up Gilbert Howard and moved his body into Villa 7B's living room. She didn't know why deducing that progression of actions made her feel even worse.

She pillowed her head in the clothing and took a deep breath. She knew one thing about the woman whose clothes these had been—she used Ivory soap, like Frankie and Connie did. This brought her a little comfort.

Holding the gun in both hands so as to be ready for any contingency, Frankie prepared herself to stay awake and alert, all through the night.

The first time she woke, her hip was giving her a hard time, and she considered leaving her hiding spot to creep into Eugene's bedroom. She knew what her father and Mrs Mooney would say if an engaged girl were to sleep in another man's bedroom, but she wondered whether they might make allowances for such behaviour in the case of a true emergency. Perhaps it might even be all right if the man put his arms around her, this once. Perhaps not. She fell back asleep before she could decide.

The second time she woke inside the closet hidey-hole, she heard a sound she was certain came from Eugene's bedroom.

A woman's sigh.

The third time Frankie woke, it was morning. She knew because birdsong travelled through the walls into her hiding place. She slipped the gun into the pocket of her green-and-blue dress. The tips of her fingers touched the dried crumbs of the sandwich she'd fed to the pigeons the day before. Otherwise, her pocket held only her engagement ring and her car key.

Frankie sat up straight in the darkness. Then she knelt on the gritty floor. How grubby her dress must be by now.

With delicacy she eased the boards out of the back of the closet. She climbed out across Eugene's shoes, disarranged after the police search the night before. Remembering the female sigh she'd heard in the middle of the night, she wasn't sure what she'd find in Eugene's dawn-lit bedroom, but he was alone now, humped up among his covers. Perhaps she'd dreamed the sigh. She stood at the foot of Eugene's bed, studying his face. Above the neck of the white cotton undershirt he slept in, his cheek looked as soft as an innocent boy's.

Her intuition over the last few hours told her that Eugene was on her side, but Frankie had never been much for trusting her feelings. Logic and common sense were her preferred guides, and both instructed her not to linger in Eugene's bedroom a moment longer, at the mercy of a man who seemed to care about Gilbert Howard's death as much as she did but who'd had in his possession the gun that had most likely killed him.

What day was this? Yesterday had been Friday, her first day as an extra in the movies. Now it was Saturday morning. She wished that Friday had turned out differently, and that Gilbert Howard were still alive. Right now she would be climbing out of her own little bed in Villa 7B with hope in her heart, anticipating her hard-earned audition for the part of a sad manicurist on Monday.

Frankie crept into the living room and peered out Eugene's front door. Dawn lit the quiet cottages and bricked pathways around Paradise Gardens. For a miracle, there was not a single policeman posted outside Eugene's Villa 7A. Frankie sidled out Eugene's door and up to her own. The plaid curtains were drawn across the living-room window. Had they taken Gilbert Howard's body away?

Of course they had. But why was there no policeman guarding the scene of the murder? Could her luck have changed as night had changed to day? Frankie remembered her little hoard of forty dollars left over after paying the Queen her rent money. She needed it now, for she had not a cent in her pocket for an escape north to Vancouver. And she knew exactly where to find it: under the sofa cushions on which Gilbert Howard's body had been sitting.

She tested Villa 7B's front doorknob. It turned. It creaked open.

At her back, so close that she felt her skirt move, somebody whispered, "Just where do you think you're going?"

CHAPTER TWO

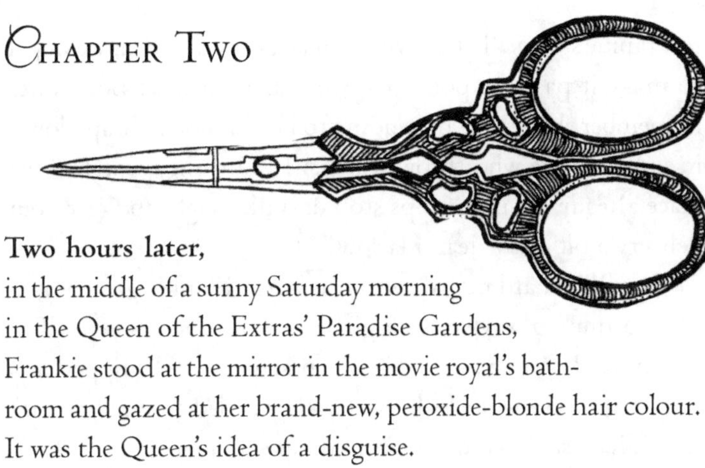

Two hours later,
in the middle of a sunny Saturday morning
in the Queen of the Extras' Paradise Gardens,
Frankie stood at the mirror in the movie royal's bathroom and gazed at her brand-new, peroxide-blonde hair colour.
It was the Queen's idea of a disguise.

It might so easily have been a policeman that found her outside
Villa 7B. If so, she would be in a police station now, pleading in
a harshly lit room for the law to believe her story. Instead, the
Queen had found Frankie and hustled her into nearby Villa 1.
Without drawing breath, the Queen had bleached Frankie's dark
hair white with the help of Billie's stolen peroxide.

Frankie leaned a little closer to the mirror. The light in the
Queen's bathroom was not good, but she believed that this new
platinum-blonde appearance suited her. Frankie murmured, *"Hey
Connie, what do you want in a hair colour?"*

If Connie had been there in the Queen's bungalow instead of
off who-knows-where, she might well have replied, *"A powerful
peroxide for a perfect blonde."*

Frankie pulled, hard enough to hurt, at her newly pale hair.
She said aloud to her reflection, "A blonde accused of murder,
pursued … but not cornered."

"A blonde who's going to make it out of town safely." The
Queen of the Extras appeared in the mirror behind her. Loretta
Desirée studied Frankie's new hair colour with an intensity equal

to Frankie's own. "If I go with you as far as the road, we ought to make it past the police to your car on Sunset Boulevard. Remember that you're pretending to be that noisy cheap blonde in 12A, the one who throws dishes. I heard they searched her place already. So if the cops stop us, talk tough, and give your delivery a bit of the Jean Harlow."

"It will be hard not to, with this hair." Frankie grinned.

"Platinum always gives a girl a certain *je ne sais quoi*." The Queen took her sharp little golden scissors and snipped at a couple of silvery-white locks so that they curled around Frankie's ears. The rest waved down around her shoulders.

Frankie said, "The important thing is for me to be *je ne sais* who."

"I guess you'll have to change your name. Can you think of a good one?"

Frankie blinked. "I was going to change my name anyway. I'm getting married."

"My goodness, how lovely," the Queen said. "What will he say when he sees your hair?"

"I can't imagine what Champ will say. Nor my dad." Frankie's hair felt light on her head. Her eyebrows stood out as clean dark lines below the silver-white locks. How many times back home had she been cast as a man because of those eyebrows? And because of her figure as well, it must be said. "I should have dyed my hair platinum years ago," she said.

"If you had, it wouldn't be much of a disguise now."

Frankie gave her new hair her fairest evaluation. She frowned. She looked good as a platinum blonde, but she also looked a lot like Frankie as a platinum blonde. "I don't know, my Queen. I'm afraid that I'd still look pretty recognizable to somebody who knows me."

"The police don't know you." The Queen inclined her head. "Maybe if we pouffed it up a little more, or bobbed it to your ears?"

She lifted Frankie's hair experimentally and raised her golden scissors to make another pass. Frankie, a little awestruck by her new platinum glamour, felt a certain resistance to cutting any of it, on the grounds that *more* beautiful hair was always preferable to *less* beautiful hair.

The Queen added, "What if we curled you up like little Shirley Temple?"

"Oh, dear! She's sweet. But please and thank you, no." Frankie felt in her dress pocket for the men's sunglasses Billie Starr had stolen for her. Were they still in one piece? She pulled out the sunglasses and put them on.

"That's better," the Queen murmured.

"The dark glasses do help. Thank goodness I'm so new in Hollywood. I wouldn't get two steps out the door if there were a photograph of me to show around."

"A photograph of you?" The Queen fell silent.

Frankie remembered the flash and pop of the camera at Central Casting. They'd taken a picture for her application form. How long did it take to develop a photograph from a glass slide? If the police were doing their job, and the Central Casting offices opened at nine, her paperwork would be in their hands already. It would be a slim little folder—she was only a first-day extra—and her photograph would be lying right on the top when the police opened it.

From Central Casting, it wasn't a long hike to Monument Studios. There, Luigi had pictures of Frankie the pigeon girl from yesterday's filming.

She experienced a fizzing, weakening sensation that began in her fingertips and spread through the rest of her. "There are at least *two* pictures of me."

"Poor Frankie." The Queen gave Frankie's shoulder a squeeze. "But they won't recognize you now. You're a young blonde woman in sunglasses, and there are thousands like you around Hollywood."

Reluctantly, Frankie disagreed. "Platinum hair is not a good enough disguise. What if you make me look older?"

"How much older?"

"Yonks. I mean decades."

"Aging makeup is the most difficult to get right." The Queen looked Frankie up and down. "With your young-gal figure, we'd have to pad you too, and even then you'd only pass at night, if the cop who talked to you was nearsighted or stewed to the gills."

And of course, she'd have to walk a little differently, remove the spring from her step and that ingénue hope from her expression. But she was an actress, wasn't she?

"I need a fairy godmother to turn me into a mouse. Or a pumpkin. Or a prince."

The Queen looked up sharply. "That's more like it," she said.

"That's an acting secret, isn't it? I need a disguise that focuses the observer on the whole rather than the changing bits of me. What if I became a nun? Then people would see the habit I wear instead of the person inside it."

"A nun?" The Queen looked doubtful. "I was going to suggest something easier. But if you really think a nun is best …" The Queen tugged a towel off the rail and wrapped it tightly around Frankie's face to make a wimple. "You can use my black robes, and we'll pin the towel into the right shape."

Frankie straightened her phony wimple and stared at herself in the mirror. Although she had grown up in a religious household, she was a most unconvincing nun. It was something about her ironic jawline, where it cut against the wimple. As well, her gaze was so secular that she'd need a lot of acting experience under her belt before she was offered a part as a *réligieuse.* For fun, she donned Billie's sunglasses again, and they both laughed. Frankie wondered if doomed people — like the French aristocrats waiting in their clammy cells to be called to the guillotine — sometimes shared a joke.

She said, "I wish Jack Benny were here to tell a funny story right now. Jack Benny wouldn't turn me in, I bet. Maybe he would change clothes with me, like Sidney Carton did in *A Tale of Two Cities.* Then I would walk away freely."

Frankie pictured herself making her way out to the Model A, her arms swinging, her manly step firm on the sun-dappled pavement.

"Now you're talking," the Queen said. "I was going to suggest just that. You're the type, with those eyebrows —"

"And my figure." She didn't want to be a man. But she reminded herself that there were many things one didn't want to do in this world.

She closed her eyes. If she had to do it, she wouldn't waste another moment. It was her fervent hope that the Queen wouldn't have a better idea once the deed was done.

She picked up the Queen's golden scissors and hooked a section of her silvery hair between her forefinger and middle finger. She'd cut her father's hair often enough. Her fingers were less steady than they'd ever been, but she could probably cut a man's hair on a ship in a gale out at sea, or perched high among the tossing branches of a tree, or under water. But cutting her father's hair underwater, she considered, would be easy compared to cutting her own. She'd have to get the Queen to help with the sides and back. Taking a deep breath, she snipped.

The little fan of platinum hair fell to the floor. She must remember to sweep up in case the police returned to search the Paradise Gardens bungalows again.

Arms folded, the Queen watched her snip. "I'm going to find you a man's suit, Frankie." The golden scissors snipped at the ends of Frankie's hair: short, shorter, shortest.

Frankie met her gaze in the mirror. "We'd better make sure it's a pretty loose fit, my Queen. I'm going to have to carry a gun."

"Walk like a man, Francesca Ray." The Queen of the Extras took another stitch in Eugene's trouser bottoms.

Eugene was, after all, only a little taller than Frankie, and the Queen was taking them up just that half-inch because, she said, the way a man's trousers cut across the instep of his shoes was more vital than money.

"I *am* walking like a man." *Exactly* like a man. There had been a dearth of boys in high school who wanted to be in plays like *Joanie Gets a Boyfriend.* Frankie's drama teacher had been very clear in her praise: when the part called for it, Frankie walked like a man. She did it now by mentally broadening her shoulders and slouching with her hands in the pockets of Eugene's jacket, which she was wearing over her dress while she waited for the trousers to be done. The Queen had agreed that the male voice was Frankie's best trick, though; she could produce a sort of gentlemanly tenor without half trying.

"Is Eugene back with my forty dollars yet? I left it right under the sofa cushion in the living room." She would be much happier when she had that money safely in hand. Frankie threw herself down at the kitchen table. "Are the trousers nearly done?"

"Invisible stitches take as long as they take, sweetie. Not much difference in height between you and Eugene, but that makes no difference to hemming time." The Queen turned a bit of trouser hem over her index finger, holding the cloth taut with her thumb and middle finger as she made her tiny stitches. "I started out as a dresser for Marie Tempest on her American tour, but I enjoyed taking understudy roles far more, and I left Miss Tempest's dressing room for the stage. I 'discovered' Gilbert Howard, you know."

In a sad sort of way, Frankie had discovered him, too: dead on the couch. She said, "Poor Gilbert Howard."

"You'd never believe it, but dear Howie was in love with me when he started out."

"Certainly I would believe it," Frankie said politely.

"We were good friends, as well, which not every one of his lady loves could claim. I met him when he was straight out of the army. He was captured, you know, by the Germans."

Connie's father had been killed in the war. However, Frankie's father Sheridan D had been too old to be called up by the time it started, and when he tried to sign up they showed him the door. Frankie tried to imagine Gilbert Howard as a soldier in the war. "I'll bet he was brave."

"Yes. And Howie looked wonderful in uniform." The Queen stretched out the unfinished cuff of Eugene's trousers and picked up her little golden scissors. "The Germans found Howie in a foxhole, declaiming Shakespeare. He didn't stay captive long, though. He escaped in the middle of the prisoners' Christmas show, dressed as the pantomime Dame, and he made his way back in skirts to England."

"Good heavens." Frankie had almost forgotten the trousers, as well as the murder accusation, so wrapped up was she in the story. "That would have made a wonderful movie, if only he could have starred in it."

Footsteps sounded lightly on the path outside Villa 1. The Queen's face lit up. "Hello, Eugene."

"What's all this?" Eugene stared from Loretta Desirée to Frankie.

"The Queen is disguising me as a man," Frankie said.

"Good heavens, Loretta."

The Queen said, "Eugene, you mustn't fuss."

"Yesterday she dressed Tom like a woman for the movies," Frankie pointed out.

Eugene said, "She's always dressing somebody as something. May I ask, are those my best trousers you're cutting up, Loretta?"

"Yes, indeed. How is the situation regarding the police?"

"It's quiet just now. The force seems to pass through in flocks, like pigeons."

Frankie asked, "Did you find my forty dollars?"

"Here, hold out your hands."

Frankie did. He took hold of her hands and studied them, much the way Frankie used to check her student's hands before letting them eat lunch.

"My Queen, you've clipped Frankie's nails short and straight. Perfectly like a man." Eugene held out his own smartly-trimmed nails and grinned at the Queen, who smiled back. A mother's smile, as if for a favourite child.

Eugene turned Frankie's hands palm up again. His own fingers were as cool and gentle as his voice. He folded her fingers around four one-dollar bills. "This is all the money I have. I couldn't find the forty dollars that you hid in the sofa cushions. Somebody must have taken your money—maybe the police, though I hate to say it. But these four dollars will get you enough gas to get you out of town. After that, you'll have to work your way back home to Vancouver."

The Queen said, "It's a sin and a shame somebody took your money, Frankie. I'm afraid that I've none to give you, for Blanche, although sorrowful over Howie's death, somehow remembered to collect every dime of the Paradise Gardens rent money."

At the loss of her forty dollars Frankie felt her disappointment like a blow between her shoulder blades. Of course the police would have taken her money—as evidence, possibly, although in the movies you learned lots about graft and corruption.

The Queen picked up the grey trousers and draped them over her shoulders. "I must press these pants before you wear them, Frankie. Doris has a working iron, and Betty's got the big ironing board." The Queen hurried out of the house.

Frankie became conscious of her half-and-half state under Eugene's steady gaze. With her man's haircut and jacket, but wearing her skirt, she must have looked a sight. "What do you think? Will I pass for a man?"

"It's not bad for a disguise," Eugene said. "I think the right word for you is *grotesque*."

"Thanks," Frankie said dryly. "I was hoping I looked like an ordinary fellow from the waist up."

"*Grotesque* is a term in Italian Renaissance studies," he elaborated. "It was used in paintings or sculpture for people or animals caught at the moment of changing from one aspect to another."

"Okay," Frankie said. "I don't mind being Italian. And a half a man. Anyway, I think the Queen has done a good job."

"She's a master of disguising other people, isn't she?"

"She seems to change one gender to the other whenever the extras need different work."

"And she also disguises the extras to help them sneak into hotels and restaurants to collect gossip for Blanche's column." He smiled. "You've seen Bruno. From the back he can pass for a child, but face-on, he looks like a small man in his thirties. But a couple of years back, when the Queen was disguising him as a little boy, he was making a hundred a week in the kiddie reels. He lasted a year."

Frankie tried to think how it would be for Bruno to live as a child for a year. "But if Bruno was making such good money, and getting steady parts in films, why did he go back to working as an extra?"

"There are problems with being somebody you're not for any length of time. Day after day, you know. It eats the soul. That's what Bruno told me, anyway."

Frankie shook her head. "Maybe it's true for Bruno. It does seem disrespectful to pay a boy well for his work, but not a man. But staying disguised wouldn't eat my soul," she said positively. "I would look on it as acting — as sustaining a part. For a successful year's run, like they do on the stage."

"But you're lucky, Frankie, because you'll never know." Eugene said. "You're going home to Vancouver. Keep a low profile, and they'll never find you on your way out of Hollywood."

"They will if the Canadian Mounties are called in. The Mounties always get their man." She raised her eyes to meet Eugene's. She held his gaze for a long moment. Then she stated the truth that revealed itself to her at the same moment she spoke the words. "I want to stay in Hollywood."

"You must not." Eugene looked away. "Who knows how long even the best disguise will stand up?"

"The Queen is an expert."

"Yes. But a burst of sunlight might illuminate the curve of your beardless jaw. Or somebody with an eye to earning a fat reward might find himself blessed with an unprecedented, superhuman instinct. Leave town, Frankie. Do it early. Do it quick."

Eugene's urgency was such that if she hadn't had such a tip-top disguise, she might have followed his advice. She said, "I'm going out into Hollywood, dressed as a man, to investigate this murder. I'll find out who killed Gilbert Howard and clear my name. Will you help?"

He took a step away from her. "If you fail, you know what it might mean."

Frankie nodded. The night before, in Eugene's closet, she had faced that particular terror dead-on. But who could fear the electric chair when the sun was shining and you were young and full of ideas? She said, "Listen. I have two clues."

Eugene, grey eyes graver than ever before, sat down at the Queen's kitchen table. He steepled his hands and then studied them. Frankie imagined the impatience that this professional police officer would feel when confronted with an amateur's ideas.

"Eugene, you must listen to what I have to say. I'm not police, but I know things about the murder that the police don't. The first clue is Billie Starr. She was there with me when I found Gilbert Howard's body on my sofa."

Eugene looked up, a spark of interest in his eyes. "I didn't know she was there."

"When she saw him dead, Billie said, 'We all know who killed him.' She knew Gilbert Howard had been murdered, even though nobody else could tell until the police showed us the bullet wound. One of us needs to question her."

Eugene shook his head. "I know Billie, Frankie. She used to live here. She always had a bottle somewhere, and——"

"Yes, she was drunk last night, too. But she seems to operate quite efficiently in that state." Frankie remembered her own panic and shock upon confronting Gilbert Howard dead on her sofa. "She reacted far more quickly than I did. Drunk as she was, she said a lovely and respectful farewell and then left before Blanche Carver or the police knew she'd been there. Maybe they would have suspected her too, although I wouldn't wish it."

"Billie wouldn't murder Gilbert." Eugene's tone was firm, as if speaking to a police subordinate who was wasting his superior officer's time on red herrings. But he had missed her point completely.

"I didn't say Billie shot him. I said she said she knows who did. That's the first clue that must be followed up." She decided to ignore his look of doubt. "Here is the second clue," she continued. "Gilbert Howard had a secret girlfriend. Among his many public girlfriends."

"Hold on, now——" Eugene began.

Frankie interrupted. "I don't suggest we interview everybody Gilbert Howard ever kissed. But this girl, who was swimming naked in the pool next door in Paradise Gardens two nights ago, was with him in the hours before he died."

"I really don't think——"

"And she may know who killed him. Or she may have killed him." She saw that he was about to interrupt again and surprised herself by holding up her hand for silence. "But listen to this, Eugene. It looked to me as if she were not simply one more star-struck girl to Gilbert Howard." She pictured the scene she, Connie, and Tom had witnessed at the swimming pool. *The kiss.* Of course Howard was an actor, and a great one, but … "*I think he was really in love with this girl, and that she knew things about his life that others didn't.*"

She hoped her guess was right. At any rate, she had him now, for Eugene nodded, and she was certain of the sincere sorrow in his grey eyes. "Frankie, you may be right."

"Good." She felt almost faint with relief. "I'll search out the golden swimmer—the girlfriend—and you go talk to Billie. I'd bet any money she's back at the brothel across the street from Monument Studios."

"No," Eugene said firmly. "I have the resources for a search, and may safely ask door-to-door as well. You may have the dubious pleasure of interviewing Billie Starr."

Even quiet men always wanted things their way. Frankie said, "Will you call in your colleagues?"

"My colleagues?"

"The police."

"No." He hesitated. "I may have inadvertently misled you, Frankie. I'm more of a private detective."

Somehow, Frankie was not surprised. She wished with all her heart that Eugene hadn't been lying to her about practically everything from the start. But she remained nearly certain that, though a liar, he was innocent of the murder. If he'd been guilty, he would not have protected her. He would have seen to it that the police found her last night and put her in jail. Eugene was not transparent, and he lied at will, but he was at least sincere. Frankie was almost sure of that, too—especially since he was not a professional actor. She refused to think more deeply about her feelings on the matter than that.

She said, "I'll meet you back here tonight. And one more thing, Eugene …"

"What?"

Frankie burst out, "*Why* didn't you call the police to dig up that body in the backyard when you said you would? If they'd taken him away, then nobody would have been able to dig him up and put him on my sofa—and I wouldn't be in this mess."

Eugene inclined his head. "Exactly who do you think knew it was Gilbert Howard buried in the backyard? Not me. Not you. All we saw was one hand uncovered in the grass and soil. We decided he was a poor anonymous fellow whose relatives had buried him there out of poverty. So I left him buried—out of kindness. Respect for an unknown dead man. I thought it would hurt nobody if he rested in peace. I did not foresee the consequences."

He looked directly at her. Frankie tried to read anything but truth in his eyes. She could not.

The door opened. The Queen returned. Across her arm hung a beautifully pressed pair of grey men's trousers. In her other hand she held a pair of men's brogues.

"Those are my shoes," Eugene said.

"Yes. And this is your suit," Frankie retorted.

"Have I any belongings left at all?" But his manner as he slipped out the door was exactly that of a man who could be relied upon to track down a movie star's nameless blonde girlfriend.

"Don't look at him like that," the Queen admonished Frankie. "Frankie, you must never fall in love in Paradise Gardens. It leads to heartbreak and discord."

"It was not that kind of look." Frankie wriggled out of her dress and into the shirt and trousers. "It was a look of hope and professional respect."

The Queen's face softened, and Frankie added, "Eugene is like your favourite child, isn't he?"

"I never had any children of my own," the Queen said. "But if Eugene were my child, he would be the apple of my eye. Poor darling!"

"Why poor Eugene?" She tugged on a pair of argyle socks that the Queen had ironed for her, and then stood while the Queen tied the brogues onto Frankie's feet. They were a little big, so she took them off again and they stuffed a bit of tissue into the toes. She tried to feel like a fellow with the weight of the world on his shoulders. The word for that, she knew from her father's sermons, was *gravitas*. "Eugene seems all right to me."

"He's lonely. Now breathe in," the Queen directed her. She lifted up the hem of Frankie's shirt and proceeded to fasten about her middle and chest a terrible elasticated bit of business that she referred to as the Xeno-Flex Combination. "Every girl was flat as Nevada for fashion a few years back," the Queen said. "If you wore a Xeno-Flex Combination, you were confident that your beads would hang straight down the front of your dress."

The Xeno-Flex Combination cut Frankie's breathing room in half and pinched her around the middle. It seemed a lot to suffer, but Frankie reminded herself of the stakes.

Standing poised for an instant on the stoop of the Queen's bungalow, Frankie felt upon her brow the Queen's parting kiss. That kiss was a sort of mother's blessing. The sensation was new to Frankie. It made her feel like the youngest brother in a fairy tale, leaving home to pursue a fate.

Gravitas. **Masculine** *gravitas.* Frankie took several solid, manly steps along the Queen's garden path, keeping an Eagle Scout eye out for the police. Through Billie's dark glasses, Paradise Gardens took on a brilliantly coloured glow and an almost Maxfield Parrish intensity. She remembered her male roles in amateur theatre back home: 'Young Blade with Tennis Racquet', 'Joanie's Boyfriend', 'Hal, the Handsome Butler in the Lady's Confidence'. She reviewed her first and most basic acting lessons, taught her by a gifted elderly director who had spent a year in New York City before washing up in Vancouver. He had insisted that it was artistic suicide to trust to inspiration to interpret a character. You had to focus on the work. She squared her shoulders, buttoned her coat around her *gravitas*, and rested her hand on the gun in her pocket.

What a hopeful young woman she had been two nights before, dancing the carioca with Eugene and trying not to lead like a man. Now she *was* a man and a lead in a criminal investigation, albeit an amateur. Hands in her pockets, her brogues loping toward Paradise Garden's central patio, she tried not to feel self-conscious of her short hair. There was a breeze around her ears, and the novelty of the sensation threatened to put her off her stride. But at the same time, she felt taller than usual, as if she were growing upward from the top of her head.

Frankie stopped at the path to her own front door.

An idea presented itself. Disguised as a man, she could slip inside Villa 7B and have a quick look for her forty dollars. Eugene might well have missed the little wad of bills, but she knew exactly where in the sofa cushions she had hidden it. How swift could she be? *As swift as thought.* Frankie tensed to make her move. Then, in the moment preceding action, she caught sight of several policemen in the hedges that bordered Paradise Gardens and the Garden of Allah. As the men peered about, their caps reminded Frankie of blackbirds hopping along the branches and searching for berries. But these were not birds, and they were not searching for berries. They were searching for her. She counted three policemen within view.

Once again, she had nearly been rash. Would she *ever* learn? Like that darned old Icarus. When Sheridan D had first told her the story, she had been disgusted with Icarus. He had wasted those beautiful wings! Now she saw how such an error might occur, all in a second's rash decision.

Striding more cautiously now, she approached Eugene's pathway.

A young woman stumbled around from behind the bungalow, then tripped and fell in a swirl of red skirts. Weeping, she sat down on the grass not six feet from Frankie.

Frankie hesitated. Red of dress and high of heel, the sorrowful woman was Marietta Valdes. Marietta had met Frankie twice before now. Would she recognize Frankie in her man's disguise? Frankie nearly turned tail and ran.

But far better to test her disguise here, where she had Eugene and the Queen to back her up or hide her again, than out in greater Hollywood and entirely on her own.

It was emphatically better to test her disguise on Marietta than on a policeman. Frankie braced herself for the test of creditable manliness, and came as close as nothing to failing it by asking Marietta, *What's wrong?* Just in time she stopped herself. A man would not ask clarifying questions. A man would act. So Frankie felt in her breast pocket for the handkerchief she knew must be there, knelt, and offered it to Marietta Valdes. Marietta accepted it, buried her beautiful face in it, and then looked up again at Frankie.

Marietta said, "The world has too few gentlemen in it." Even with her mascara smudged beneath her eyes, her superior bone structure shone in the early afternoon light. With the handkerchief she wiped at the smudges under her eyes and said, "I'm sorry. No, I'm not. I was overcome by sorrow at the death of a friend."

Gilbert Howard. Marietta's face buckled into tears again. Frankie tried and failed to figure out how anybody could wear a twisted, weeping face and still look beautiful. "I'm sorry for your loss. I was so sad to hear the news as well."

"Thank you. Howie was the only person in the whole world on my side. He tried and tried to help me in my struggles to direct films. I suppose that seems crazy to you." Marietta blew her nose gracefully. "You look like an actor. Are you?"

Frankie shook her head. If only she were. And she would have been this coming Monday, if only the world had revealed itself a friendlier, fairer place.

She cursed herself for breaking character and swore not to do so again.

"No, I'm not an actor."

"It's hard to believe."

She held out a hand to help Marietta to her feet. Marietta rose like a flag on a pole and then tottered in her heels on the grass. She slipped one shoe off and then the other. She looked deep into Frankie's eyes and added, "You should be an actor. Any professional can see that you've got that something."

You've got that something. How Frankie had always yearned for somebody to say exactly that to her, and not only to Connie. She wanted to laugh, or possibly cry—yes, sit down on the grass, bury her hands in her face, and weep for her lost chance at her audition for a role as a sad little manicurist in Samson's new epic *The Emperor of New York.*

Instead, she said, "Thank you, Miss Valdes."

Marietta stepped barefoot onto the pathway, a shoe in each hand. Her gaze was searching. "You know me, but I don't know you."

"Everybody knows you, Miss Valdes," Frankie said. "My name is Franklin. Call me Frank."

"But Frank who?"

Criminy. She couldn't give her own surname, *Ray.* She might as well tear her off her disguise and step out into the world as her murder-suspect self. At a moment like this, she certainly missed Connie. *Hey, Connie, what do you want in a man's name?* But instead of Connie, Frankie's father Sheridan D whispered in her ear: *Here's a good name for you, Frankie. Solid, and built on classical lines.*

"I'm Frank Achilles."

"A good name for a knight in shining armour."

"Thanks," Frankie said. Too late she recognized the unsuitability of Homer's *Achilles* for a name. Achilles was a hero, of course, but he had sulked in his tent. And he was certainly not a gentleman. But it was too late to switch to *Frank Ulysses,* and anyway Ulysses, with all his clever tricks, was no gentleman either. "Keep the handkerchief, won't you?"

Marietta said, "A fellow like you, with those cheekbones, your moonlight head of hair, and your slender build?" She touched red-tipped fingers to the lapel of Frankie's coat, and Frankie was grateful for the flattening security of the Xeno-Flex Combination. "Frank, any director worth his salt would see the possibilities in you. If you're not an actor, what are you?"

"I'm ..." What was Frank Achilles? Frankie pondered the question. What were men, anyway? Ministers, roaring and hiding their sherry. Insurance men like Champ, pink-faced and close to the money. Haberdashers. Shoe salesmen. *Detectives.* She grinned. "Well, maybe I'm an actor of a sort after all."

"Of course you are." Marietta smiled, although her eyes were still a little pink about the edges. "I saw it immediately. It's a director's instinct. If only I had a movie to direct."

"I believe," Frankie said politely—no, *with chivalry*—"I believe you would make a fine motion picture director, Miss Valdes."

"Do you?" Marietta took a step closer. "That's encouraging to hear. Very encouraging indeed. I hope we meet again, Frank Achilles. With Gilbert Howard dead, I need all the discerning actors in this godforsaken town that I can get on my side." Without a goodbye, Marietta Valdes strolled away, swaying like an expensive ship crossing the swell of the sea.

Frankie watched the actress walk away in the direction of Sunset Boulevard. She had two successive thoughts. The first was that she had passed the test of believability. Her disguise had held up: even at close quarters, Marietta had believed that Frankie was Frank Achilles.

Her second thought was that as soon as she got out of these men's clothes, she really had to learn to walk like Marietta Valdes.

As the distance between them grew, Frankie put her hands deep into her pockets and rocked, manlike, on the heels of her brogues. Thus, she was completely in character to receive Marietta's backward look, a glance pulled straight out of Cupid's quiver and fletched in gold. In return, Frankie touched her forehead in a male salute to Beauty.

Graceful in bare feet, Marietta swung her red shoes by their straps and sailed away through Paradise Gardens. Once the actress had disappeared from view, Frankie did not hesitate. She headed off in pursuit of the truth — to be exacted from Billie Starr.

Chapter Three

"Brother, do you know a gal with a heart of gold?" Frankie sang in her best tenor imitation as she drove up sunny Sunset Boulevard in her father's reliable Ford Model A. The solid brogues she wore made a difference: they rode heavy on the gas and light on the brake. It was not that Frankie had become a better driver because she looked like a man. She might have been sitting with a man's confidence, and she might have had her elbow hooked out the driver's window in the manner of a man, but these were part of the professional actress's toolbox. The real difference was that she sported trousers rather than the usual skirt. The first time Frankie had seen Katherine Hepburn wearing trousers in *Movie Mirror* the previous year, she'd been startled. But now she

understood what Blanche Carver, in her white trouser suits, must already know: trousers aided competence and freedom. As well, there was more freedom in the knee and thigh area than Frankie would ever have expected from a simple pair of grey twill trousers.

"*She'd turn a king's head, that's what I've been told ... Hey de hoo de hee ...*" She trailed off in the middle of the chorus of 'Dora Heart'.

"We all know who killed him." Frankie echoed Billie's words, spoken out of the blue not long after the two of them had found the body on Villa 7A's living-room sofa.

Billie was a drunk and lived in a brothel.

Still, she had seemed so sure.

Frankie hoped it would not be difficult to negotiate a meeting with Billie Starr. She only needed to ask the girl that one question: *Who killed Gilbert Howard?* Frankie pushed the Model A a little harder, made a U-turn, and pulled up in front of the brothel. She drove up onto the curb and then down, with a hearty slap and a scrape of tire that told her she'd landed accurately. She hauled on the brake and considered swinging lightly out of the window of the Model A without opening the door, but decided it would be too conspicuous and exited the car in the usual manner. She strode beneath the palm trees, up the walk toward the Spanish-style mansion that was really a brothel, her trousers flapping, her short platinum hair riffling in the afternoon breeze, and one hand in her pocket to cradle the gun.

She knocked on the brothel's door. The boy who opened it reminded her of Pats, her cheeky paperboy back home. Behind him, a tidy entry hall glowed with natural light. At the far end of the hall, a stairway curved up to a landing.

"I'm here to see one Billie Starr," Frankie said.

"Best of luck to you, young man," the boy responded cheekily.

Frankie hid her smile. "Go polish an apple, kid," she said.

Still barring her way, the boy looked her up and down. "You're an actor, aren't you? Jeepers, you look like one. That hair!"

"Sure I am, kid." She grinned back. "May I step inside, then?"

He salaamed. "You can do handstands for all I care, mister. But you'll have to get by the manager to go upstairs."

A woman in a brown suit entered the lobby. Anywhere else, Frankie would have pegged her as a manager of a high-priced dress shop, or maybe a legal secretary.

The madam shooed the boy away. "Scamp. Go make yourself a sandwich." She smiled after him. "He's the apple of my eye, but he's no angel."

"Those are the best kind. They're independent thinkers," Frankie said courteously.

She followed the madam into the lobby. What with the large electric candelabra and clerestory lighting over the stairs, the place was so bright and modern that you had to wonder whether it made a difference doing what must be very unpleasant work in a building designed on such pleasant lines. She said, "My name is Frank Achilles. I'd like to see one of your girls for a moment, if I may."

"Of course, Mr Achilles. I'll need your reference." The madam looked over her shoulder at the door through which the boy had left. "I sure hope that kid doesn't mess up my kitchen. He makes more of a disaster putting together one sandwich than a raccoon in a trash can."

"My reference?" Frankie touched the gun in her pocket.

"A written reference." The madam's smile was patient — Frankie guessed she'd explained these procedures before. "It protects the girls, *you* understand. And cash on the barrelhead, of course, unless the studio is covering your tab."

The studio! Paying for prostitute services. Good heavens. Frankie felt out of her depth. "I want to talk to her, that's all. She's a friend of mine and I need to ask her a question."

"What sort of question?" The madam asked evenly. "And which girl do you mean?"

Frankie shifted her shoulders under her jacket. With no reference and almost no money, she saw two choices ahead and approaching quickly, like Burma-Shave ads on the side of the road. First, she could leave and wait outside until Billie emerged on her own. Or she could pull out her gun and threaten the woman with it until she produced Billie. Frankie doubted that a madam would call the police to a brothel, but a person who operated outside the law might herself be armed. In such a case, there might ensue complications involving gunplay for which Frankie was not prepared.

Frankie knew from her reading of *The Odyssey* that the best, most intelligently concocted lie was the one the woman would want to believe. A lie that wouldn't get the madam into trouble.

Remembering the young boy's conviction that she looked like a movie actor, Frankie said, "Ma'am, I'm the new lead actor in King Samson's movie *The Emperor of New York*. I won't need a letter for your file because pretty soon my face will be on every billboard in town. I'm going up those stairs to see Billie Starr for a minute, but I guarantee it's not a paying trip. All right?"

"Oh." The woman rolled her eyes. "Billie Starr. *That* one. I truly have no objection. Go on up and do your worst."

"Which door is Billie's?"

"Room 11. I don't think it'll help you any, though."

"Thank you kindly."

Frankie took the curved stairs two at a time to the floor above, the gun in her pocket bumping against her leg. At the top of the stairs Frankie came face to face with Mae West's clever leer gazing out from a line of framed posters that brightened the shadowy hall: Moira Shearer, Clark Gable, Leslie Howard, and, of all people, Greta Garbo—dressed in men's clothes as the star of *Queen Christina.* Frankie gave Queen Christina an Eagle Scout salute. She ventured along the corridor and counted up the numbers. A window at the end of the hallway looked out across the Spanish tiled roof. Room 12 was to the left of the window, and 11 to the right. She knocked and tried the knob, but the door to Room 11 was locked tight against her—or rather, against somebody. How odd it was that a prostitute should lock her door. She knocked again and then hammered on the door, but there was no answer.

Would nothing ever be easy? Frankie gave the knocking a rest and leaned against the window at the end of the hallway to rub her sore knuckles. She craned her neck out the corridor window and made out the side view of Room 11's open window sash. She cast her gaze further, over the angled, red-tiled roof and across Sunset Boulevard. There stood the angels on each side of the Monument Studios gates. It seemed insulting and unfair that yesterday she'd been inside that studio, in front of the cameras, and now she was bruising her knuckles on a brothel bedroom door.

She hammered a little louder, and then louder still. A voice from a nearby room shouted, "Stop your racket, noisy!"

"Sorry!" Frankie had hoped to keep the discussion one-on-one with Billie, but as the door to Room 12 opened at her back, she saw that even the smallest actions in a place like this would have consequences. A girl stood in the doorway, fresh in a blue gingham housedress, as if she'd just come from hanging up the wash. The line from the old poem chanted inside Frankie's head nonsensically: *The gingham dog and the calico cat, side by side on the table sat.*

She glanced from Frankie to the door. "Brother, have you got your wires crossed. *That* one never answers."

"She's inside, then?" Frankie looked from the girl in gingham to Billie's door. "Why doesn't she answer?"

The gingham girl inclined her head. "She's got some kind of a deal with the management. A friend in high places, if you ask me." She looked over her shoulder into her room. "Gotta go. See you, handsome. Ask for Maggie next time."

The door to Room 12 closed, and Frankie heard shouts from inside. The argument worried Frankie, because when you're wearing the colours and shape of a man, you have to be ready to do a man's work. How likely was it, she wondered, that at some point she would be called on to use her fists to defend a woman? Frankie knew enough to keep her wrist straight when she released a punch. Champ had taught her to do so in a playful sparring match one evening while they listened to the radio, but she was certain there was no good substitute for the fisticuffs boys learned in the rough-and-tumble schoolyard.

The shouts grew fiercer in volume inside Room 12. Maggie the gingham girl seemed to give as good as she got — so far. Frankie took a deep breath preparatory to breaking into Room 12, but all at once the racket stopped, and somebody — the gingham girl, she was certain — laughed once, as if she had won a point in a long tennis set.

Frankie returned to the problem at hand: Billie didn't answer her knock. And Frankie was not capable of breaking down a door. Again, she remembered the tears, like pearls, on Billie's cheek the evening they'd found Gilbert Howard's body. *We all know who killed him.* Billie had been drunk, of course, but not too drunk for sense. And she might have been sobered, perhaps, by the shock of the great actor's death. At any rate, drunk or sober, she was Frankie's best clue. If Frankie couldn't get through to Billie, all she had was the nameless golden swimmer who had kissed Gilbert Howard a few hours before he was shot. She wondered how Eugene Ellery was coming along in his search for Gilbert Howard's mysterious girlfriend.

Frankie craned out of the window next to Billie's closed door. She scanned about the building and down through the palm trees to the ground two stories below. If she climbed outside the building to reach Billie's window, she'd have to rely on her sense of balance and good luck. If luck deserted her—as it had been doing off and on with devastating consequences for the last twenty-four hours—she was plenty high enough to fall and break her neck. She pictured herself falling two stories down to lie crumpled in the brothel's garden beneath the rattling palms. She imagined Marietta Valdes, of all people, bending over her, a sad and final farewell in her eyes. Frankie produced some good final words: "'Twill serve, 'twill serve."

But when she imagined the headline—*Murderess Francesca Ray Falls to Her Death: The Justice of Fate*—the unfairness so infuriated her that she was ready to give up on the whole project rather than give Blanche Carver the satisfaction of writing such a phony obituary. But maybe she could make the climb without disaster. After all, she had taught as a substitute for Millicent Biggs in girls' Phys Ed class. During that time, she had climbed the ropes to the roof of the school gymnasium and lived to descend them again. Her balance was good. She only lacked rooftop experience.

Frankie got her hip up on the sill and swung herself out of the corridor window onto a narrow tiled ledge on the outside of the Spanish-style mansion. She found a foothold on the sloping tiles—not only sloping, but loose as well. All at once the enterprise seemed a foolish, daring deed, and she found herself grinning like a pirate. Like the great star Douglas Fairbanks in all his swashbuckling glory.

She spared a glance across the road for the angels at the gates to Monument Studios. *Look, girls, I'm as tall as you are.* Between the studios and the mansions, cars rambled and raced along Sunset Boulevard, which made her dizzier than altitude alone could achieve. But she would never have slipped had it not been for Marietta Valdes.

On the far side of Sunset Boulevard, unmistakable in red even from that distance, the actress stood on the sidewalk outside the studio, looking up at the roof of the Spanish-style brothel. She shaded her eyes with her hands. Frankie supposed that Marietta might be looking at something else in Frankie's general direction, but there was nothing more likely to catch the eye than a man in a grey suit sidling along the rooftop toward an open window.

It was a dicey moment, and she nearly lost her balance. She recovered herself and sent Millie Biggs and the Phys Ed students at Magee Junior Secondary School a prayer of thanks. She slid a few more unsteady steps along the roof tiles, hanging onto the eaves with both hands and cursing her stiff and slippery men's brogues, as well as the darned constricting Xeno-Flex Combination around her chest.

Down in the street, Marietta was making her way through the door into the studio. Was she going to call the police?

Frankie released the near edge of the corridor window with her right hand and grasped the eave with her left. She gripped the bit of the casement window nearest the wall and peered inside. She crouched down, got one leg over the windowsill, lost her balance completely, and fell through Billie's window.

The casting call is murder

COMING SOON FROM

PULP LITERATURE PRESS

WHAT KIND OF STORY?

AJ Lee

AJ Lee is a Canadian writer without a long and interesting list of careers, a Twitter account, or a cat. You can find her at ajlee.ca.

What Kind of Story?

Once upon a time, a young person lived with their parents in a narrow townhouse. Their parents believed the young person loved them, as parents often do, but our young person resented them, as all grown children will. They—let's call them Jacky—wanted to make their own way in the world. They wanted to build their own life.

But you know that, of course. And you know what it's like out here in once-upon-a-time. So you know our Jacky was on Tinder. Or Bumble, or maybe even OKCupid. Whatever. And they found the perfect match.

They didn't message The Match right away. They screencapped the page and sent it to their best friend to make sure it wasn't too good to be true. They weren't stupid. But by the time they had composed the perfect reply, the profile was gone.

Oh, they wailed and they cried, they fumed and they smoked. They checked the app again and again and again. The first night, there was nothing, and their mother said there were plenty of fish in the sea if only you would do something about your hair. The second night, there was nothing, and their father told them to be quiet down there and put out that fucking cigarette, you ingrate.

On the third night, Jacky's best friend texted: the prince was having a ball. Maybe The Match would be there? The Match's photo — all hair and haze and sharp glittering eye — certainly looked like the sort of friend a prince might have.

Jacky laced up their sneakers and left through the back door. The sun hadn't quite set, the air was humid and reeking, and our young person was going to the ball. They took the streetcar, dropping their last token into the machine.

A reveller in a lopsided mask let our Jacky in. Jacky, bare-faced and hoodie-clad, felt naked, but they walked through the party toward the throne, shoving past goblins and fairies and humans dressed up as goblins and fairies. Someone put a red cup in their hand, but it's like I said earlier: Jacky's not stupid. They didn't drink.

"Hey," the prince said. They were gorgeous. Princely, even. "Did someone get you a drink?"

"I'm looking for someone," Jacky said.

"Maybe they're here," the prince said. "It's a pretty big party."

"Maybe."

"Have another drink."

Jacky's best friend had taught them this spell: incant "I'm good," lift your cup in the air.

The prince nodded. "Stick around. Maybe your match will show."

Jacky stayed for three nights. The first night, they watched from the corner. The second night, a fairy gave them a mask, and they danced. The third night, they drank, and it was fine.

The prince smiled when they saw Jacky drinking. "I guess your match didn't come," they said. "Sorry." The sun was coming up. The prince looked a little tired. "But you had a good time, right?"

The mask hid Jacky's face.

Had they? They'd missed three calls and ignored eleven texts, but did that mean they'd had fun?

The dawn's sickly light caught the prince's statement necklace. They saw Jacky looking.

"Here," they said, unfastening it. "Take it. A party favour." The metal was still warm from their collarbone. Jacky fastened it around their own neck.

"It's magic," the prince said offhandedly. "It'll help you find your match."

Jacky stepped out into the bright day, their mouth sticky and stale. The necklace pointed them to a Tim Horton's, where they spent their last few dollars on a coffee, the amulet humming against their chest. It led them into the foyer of an office building, then out again into the alley behind. It thrummed as they passed dumpsters smelling of old fish and lemongrass.

In another story, our hero would be meeting their best friend for smokes in this alley, taking a break from their unpaid internships, breathing in the stink but knowing it was better than making small talk with temporary co-workers.

In this story, Jacky's best friend had texted them and they hadn't even looked at it. They were digging through their bag for their phone when they heard a 'hey' from the trash.

"Did you get a donut?" A small head—furry, black and white, beady eyed—popped out of the dumpster. "Can I have a bite?"

"No," Jacky said, since they hadn't, and even if they had they weren't about to give it to a raccoon.

Well. Maybe they would've. They weren't stupid, and in this kind of story you're expected to share what you have. They didn't offer it their coffee, though, even though it was a double-double and the raccoon might've liked it.

"Too bad," it said. Jacky stepped closer, looked into its dark shiny eyes. "What?"

"Am I supposed to kiss you or something?" Jacky asked.

"I'd rather you didn't."

"Yeah."

"I'm not, like, enchanted." It shrugged skinny shoulders. "That's what you're asking, right? If I'll turn into a princess after true love's kiss?"

"I'm looking for someone." Jacky resumed digging through their bag for their phone.

"Why are you asking me?"

"The prince's amulet pointed me here."

"Oh! In that case," the raccoon said, then dived into the dumpster. Jacky waited. When it emerged, it was holding a bulging cloth sack in its sharp, awful hands. Jacky tried to take the bag, but the raccoon held on.

They stared at the raccoon. It grinned back. "Come on, don't pretend like you don't know the rules. I'm not gonna just give you something. You wouldn't even share your donut."

"I don't have a donut," they said. "I guess you can have my coffee?"

"Caffeine makes me feel funny," it said. "I want to come with you. I want to ride on your shoulder and hold on to your hair, and when you find your match, I want to move in with you and eat at your table and sleep in your bed."

"Ha ha," said our hero.

It clutched the bag to its patchy coat. "I'm serious," it said. "Living in dumpsters isn't all it's cracked up to be."

"I don't even know what's in the bag."

"What kind of story do you think this is? Whatever I have is going to help you. The amulet sent you here, didn't it?"

The amulet vibrated gently under Jacky's shirt. "Fine."

It climbed to the lip of the dumpster. "Pick me up."

Jacky shuddered, but they stuck their arm out. It shifted the dingy bag into its mouth then clambered up Jacky's forearm, claws digging into flesh. It was heavy.

Once it was firmly on Jacky's shoulder, it passed the bag out in front of their face. Our hero was, by this point, totally used to the stench of this story, and they barely clocked the smell. They took the bag.

Inside were a handful of shiny stones and a broken restaurant pager, the kind where you press a button and a tacky coaster flashes.

"You little shit," they said to the raccoon.

"What?" it said, whiskers quivering against their ear. "Take one."

Jacky plucked a gem between finger and thumb.

"Red, eh? Interesting. You sure?"

"Uh," Jacky said. "Sure."

"Okay," it said, like it wasn't. "Add it to the amulet."

Jacky held the amulet in one hand and the gem in the other. Turned each over.

"Do I have to tell you everything?" the raccoon said.

"I can figure it out," Jacky lied.

The raccoon's little hands skittered across their shoulder and pulled the amulet away.

Jacky had no idea what it did — and honestly, neither do I. But the stone had become part of the amulet, and it was vibrating harder than ever, tugging our hero in a new direction: out of the alley, into the street. People in other stories were heading to work, suits and heels and that fresh deodorant smell. Jacky watched them and felt tired and broke, and tired of being broke and tired. They hadn't brushed their teeth in three days, and hand sanitizer is not a substitute for a shower. And now they had a greasy raccoon nestled in the crook of their neck.

They were tempted, briefly, to step into another story: lean against the wall, take a break from all this, check their phone. But the weight of all those unanswered messages was heavier than the raccoon.

They followed the amulet's lead. They had to cut through brambles and answer riddles and walk over glass and all that, but it was cheaper than an Uber.

The amulet stilled at an overpass.

"Look," said the raccoon.

There was someone crouched in the shadows. Jacky pulled out their phone to see if they matched The Match.

But you listen to a lot of stories, don't you? You pay attention to these things.

How many days had it been? How often had that phone buzzed? Of course it was dead.

"You know," said the raccoon, "I'm not so sure this is the right place."

"What?" Jacky hissed. "Why not?"

"You never just get a bad feeling about shit?"

Jacky always had a bad feeling about everything. This was no different. They took a step forward.

"Fine," it said. "Don't listen to me. Not like I've been nothin' but helpful." It leapt off Jacky's shoulder. Before scampering away, it turned its sharp face, eyes catching the light. "If it does work out, let me know. We still have that deal."

The person under the bridge noticed them, showed a glint of teeth in a handsome grin.

"Hey," Jacky managed.

"Hey yourself."

"What are you doing here?"

Another glint. "I'm the bridge troll. Toll is a kiss."

Jacky was hooked.

For their first date, they brought Jacky to their condo, served risotto and fresh-baked bread. The next morning, Jacky woke in their bed. They'd left a note: "Off to work," it read. "Stay till I get back, my delicious one."

Our hero did, since they had nowhere else to be and since no one had called them 'delicious' before. They rolled out of bed, thinking they might plug in their phone and look at some of those messages.

Their cable wasn't in their bag.

Whatever. They'd found The Match.

That evening was a brand-new date: a new meal, a new night, a new note the next morning.

On the third evening Jacky said, "Let's go out tonight." They were, it had to be said, getting a little bored.

"I'd rather not," The Match said, with a lascivious wink.

"I'll pick up some Thai, then."

But The Match touched Jacky's wrist with hot fingertips, and it was like they'd been frozen in place.

"Stay," The Match said, running their fingers toward the bend in Jacky's elbow. "I want to cook with you."

They were terribly beautiful. Jacky stayed.

The next morning the door was locked from the outside. Jacky didn't even know condos *had* doors that locked from the outside.

What would you do? Your phone's dead, you're locked in a tower. No one is looking for you.

Our Jacky sat on the balcony, twelve storeys up, and smoked the butts of cigarettes from the ashtray.

They're not stupid. They're not the kind of person who thinks, This was an accident, a strange yet innocent mistake!' Even if the mistake maker was The Match.

They flicked the still-lit smoke off the edge.

When The Match got home, they slipped through the door and locked it behind them, not even stopping to put down the grocery bag. Jacky was sitting at the kitchen island.

"Hey, sweets."

"You locked me in," Jacky said.

"It was an accident," they said. "A strange yet innocent mistake."

They kissed Jacky's open mouth, and Jacky believed them. They're not stupid. But this was The Match.

The next morning there was no note.

Oh, Jacky was pissed. They tore through the house like a cornered cat, trying to find enough rope to get to the next balcony. Instead, they found their phone cable: cut in half and left in two coils at the bottom of the linen closet.

That night, Jacky tried to tell The Match their friends would be worried.

"Worried they haven't heard from you in a week? That's not so unusual for you, is it?" The Match walked across the room. "Come on, cupcake. Isn't this fun? Like Beauty and the Beast?" Their palms shimmered with the olive oil they'd been massaging into kale. Jacky imagined those oil-slicked hands on their body, rubbing dressing into flesh.

Another glint of teeth. "I can make it more fun if you want."

Jacky launched themself forward, taking the troll's thick neck between their hands. They sputtered, shoved at Jacky's shoulders. Our hero planted a firm knee in their stomach, felt their throat move as they tried to retch.

"Where's the key?" Jacky's spittle hit the troll's face. "Where's the fucking key?"

They coughed. Jacky squeezed harder.

The troll opened their red-rimmed eyes and laughed. They shoved Jacky, hard enough that they lost their grip and went stumbling. The troll advanced, teeth glinting, as Jacky scrambled toward the bedroom.

"You're just hangry," the troll said. "I'll make you some Kraft Dinner to tide you over until supper, okay?"

Jacky slammed the bedroom door, fumbled at the lock with shaking hands.

We all know, of course, that it wouldn't matter: the troll had all the keys.

"I'm not mad, okay?" the troll said through the door. "You just need to forgive yourself. Accept other people into your life."

Jacky said nothing. Eventually the troll said, "I'll leave supper in the fridge. Let me know when you're feeling better."

In another story, Jacky's lips pull away from their teeth and their sobs turn to snarls. They transform into a bear, smash down the door, eat the troll before the troll can eat them.

In another story, hair explodes from Jacky's head and they let it down, and their real match climbs it and rescues them.

In another story Jacky wakes up from this.

But we know this isn't that kind of story.

Jacky unclenched their lips, uncurled their fists, and dumped their backpack on the floor. Pawed through old receipts and crumbling

Advils, stained the troll's rug with an open chapstick. Once everything else was pushed aside, Jacky was left with the raccoon's bag.

The gems glittered like costume jewellery, but the broken restaurant pager looked a lot less broken. Jacky pressed the buttons. Then they went to the balcony.

They'd only just lit up when they heard claws against the railing. The raccoon pulled itself over the ledge.

"You found your match?" it said. "You got a nice meal made up for me? It was a hell of a climb getting up here, you know."

Jacky ashed out the cigarette.

"No meal?" It looked at them hard. "Oh. No match." It shrugged. "I did say I had a bad feeling about that troll."

"Can you get me out of here or not?"

"Why do you keep asking me for shit like that? This ain't one of those stories where I tell you you're a princess from space or something. I'm just a raccoon."

Jacky squatted and looked the raccoon right in its beady little eyes. There was a beauty to them, up that close. Like gems.

"Please help me," our hero said. "Please."

The raccoon chittered. "Fine, fine." It disappeared off the ledge.

Moments later, the troll started shouting. When Jacky heard the front door open, they slipped out of the bedroom. And when they peered down the building's bright hallway and saw the troll chasing the raccoon with a broom, they dashed out the door, down the stairs, and on to the street.

Eventually the raccoon caught up. "What colour gem are you gonna try now?"

"None," Jacky said.

"Oh, come on. What kind of story do you think this is? You gotta try three times at least."

Jacky shrugged. "I think I'm done with stories."

Back through the brambles, backwards riddles answered, broken glass unbroken.

In another story, Jacky's best friend would be enchanting a wedding carriage or maybe getting their eyes pecked out.

But like Jacky said, they're done with stories. They buzzed up to their friend's apartment, and their friend hugged them tight even with the raccoon on their shoulder. When they pulled away, they looked Jacky in the face, and Jacky said, "I need your help."

They let them in.

What would you do? You go on this journey, and it brings you right back to your best friend. You find what you already had — but honestly, Jacky'd been looking for their match all this time, and look where it had gotten them.

What would you do? Trade the prince's amulet back to them for their family's cottage up north? Sell the raccoon's gems and get your MBA?

Jacky moved into their best friend's apartment, and eventually the two of them found a nice two-bedroom in the west end.

I know you're expecting a happy-ever-after, but that's for the old days, when ever after was short and happiness was a full belly and a house with a chimney. Nowadays the best we can hope for is happy for now, happy this year, and happy memories ever after.

And the raccoon?

The raccoon got a little dog bed in Jacky's room, which was as close to their promise as this life was to the one Jacky had been looking for. And, yeah, our hero didn't find exactly what they were looking for. Honestly, what kind of story did you think this was?

LITTLE SNOWFLAKE GIRLS

Dawn Lo

Dawn Lo *is a Hong Kong–Canadian writer based in Singapore. She holds an MA in Creative Writing from LASALLE College of the Arts. Her work has appeared or is forthcoming in* Queenmob's Tea House, The Malahat Review, *and* Asian Cha Journal, *among others.*

Little Snowflake Girls

Every weekday, after I make dinner, I wait at the parlour window for Big Sister to come home from work. Today, I have an even better time of it because snow has fallen. This is my fifth winter in Toronto, after Mother, Sister, and I emigrated from Hong Kong. Snow has become my absolute favourite thing.

In the afternoon, the neighbourhood children dance and make snow angels like little darlings. When the sun sets and the sky greys into a frown, they take their laughter home. I wish they'd stayed for me to watch into the evening, but now, at least, I can come out from behind the curtain. I can press my cheek against the chilly glass. Mother saw on TV that if you lick frozen doorknobs, your tongue gets stuck. What about windows? I lean against the cold windowpane, my nipples pricking, and I giggle. Steam forms on the glass around my mouth like a kiss. My tongue darts gecko-like against ice; then I launch myself back. Still intact!

Last winter, I had gone outside on a snowy day like this. Only one boy from next door was out playing. I felt safe to go because I'd watched him grow up, so we were friends. He looked eight and a half. I nuzzled his little nose to get a better look at his green eyes that shone like Tai Tam Reservoir on a sunny day. His father found us. He asked me how old I was. He had to ask again when I didn't answer, not because I don't understand English, but because my thumping heart made it too hard to focus. When I told him nineteen, he frowned and took his boy away.

Mother and Sister said I was lucky it was the father who found me; mothers are less forgiving. But also, maybe, it could have been unlucky. I don't know what that means, but Mother insisted that I be more careful: "Little snowflake girls ought to stay home." That night, I imagined being the boy's mother, holding his hand in bed because he was frightened. Or being the man's wife, lying next to him, his body warm, a force, and then I had to go downstairs for some water.

I understand, now, I am too old to play with children. I watch from inside. They don't see me behind the lace curtain. This is not hard; I am tall but very skinny, all limbs. When I fold up onto the bay window, I might look like an ironing board to them. Anyway, children only have eyes for the cotton clumps, the sparkle of sun on the white. I can understand if they don't care to see me here.

Mother calls from the next room. "Are you wearing enough, Daughter?"

"Yes!" I say, though my pyjama shirt and pants are thin cotton. I spin and spin until the blur of grey and blue curtains, carpets, and chairs mixes into one. Mother is very smart. She learns many things from TV. From the moment she opens her eyes, the TV flickers on too. Right now, she is crocheting a sweater in her wheelchair, and the TV in her room is on Fairchild, our only Cantonese channel. Mother doesn't speak a lick of English. She cares only for her old life.

Beep beep-beep goes the jingle for the evening Hong Kong news. "Governor Chris Patten has called an inquiry," says the

TV, "for the New Year's stampede that took the lives of over twenty people."

I remember in Hong Kong when I could walk to the market by myself, the crowd would just sweep you up. Heat radiated from chests and arms so close you could lick beads of their sweat, and I would wonder who the well-dressed man in a suit was going to steam flounder for, or where the old lady pushing a trolley of cardboard boxes was headed. I never liked going out but, somehow, I liked losing myself in the crush of people.

The front door opens. Sister's home!

We eat dinner in the kitchen always. The dining room is Mother's bedroom. Mother wheels herself to the little round table next to the refrigerator. I tell Sister to sit, though she tries to help. It's not only that I want her to rest after work, it's because I have my way in the kitchen, of setting the table and serving the dishes I keep warm in the rice cooker.

Mother breathes in the fragrant Thai Jasmine rice as she savours a mouthful. "I hardly ate rice like this growing up. Only times were when your grandfather won big at mah-jong dens. He'd come home in the middle of the night stinking of cigarettes and cheap perfume, but there would also be the scent of steamed black-bean ribs on rice. Us children would rush over sleepily, but I was always last! Because my leg —"

"Your leg, your polio. Mother," Sister says, "how can we forget?"

"Still no sympathy from you."

"I have *plenty* of sympathy. Just no patience."

"Let her tell," I say to Sister.

"I'll never understand why you indulge her like this." Sister pinches my cheek but turns to Mother nicely.

"I like to hear." I don't say it's because I know the relief of having someone listen.

"Ah this leg: last to the dinner table, last to the playground, last to be married. Your father was the only good man. He could see I was a nice girl, he didn't care a flip about the leg! On our wedding day, he borrowed his wealthy uncle's car — a red convertible — and carried me from the flat all the way to the car." Mother exhales. "My girls, you must marry a *real* gentleman, even if you have to wait — "

"Thirty-two years like you," Sister says, yawning. "I'm almost there. See what a good girl I've been, taking your advice?"

As she gets up, I ask, "Why were you so late? Even for a Friday, you're never this late."

She winks. "Tell you later."

Sister is on her bed, brushing her hair when I go say good night. She tells me to sit on the floor in front of her, so she can brush mine.

"You should grow it out." She pieces through my chin-length hair with uneven tufts, especially in the back. It's difficult to cut straight lines while leaning over the bathroom sink.

"Or," she continues, "let's go to the hairdressers. Get someone to fix this up."

"I'm fine cutting it myself."

"The place I go to is wonderful."

"I don't want to."

"You've got to try." Sister puts the brush down. "Try to go out."

"I do! I push Mother around the neighbourhood. Sometimes we go as far as the pond to feed the ducks."

"I mean to be with people."

"What were you going to tell me?" I ask quickly. "At dinner. You said later."

"Oh, yes." Sister swings her legs around and lies down. "I'm bringing a friend home for dinner tomorrow. Don't worry about cooking, we'll get takeout. Want to try pizza again?"

"Friend?"

"Or should we get the beef noodles you like?"

"What friend?"

"Just someone from work."

"She's an engineer?"

"He," she says, pulling up the covers, "is, yes."

"A *man*." I wheel around to look at her.

"Oh stop it, you sound just like Mother. He is very nice. You'll both love him."

I say nothing. Sister mumbles sleepily about him, how he's older and funny, but I don't hear much because, all of a sudden, I'm trembling. I grip my hands together. I roll segments of my finger bones until I want to cry out.

Sister has fallen asleep. She works so hard to make money for the three of us. I turn off the light and go to close the curtains. Outside, the snow and the moon dye everything the same colour. If I blur my eyes a little, it looks like there are no other houses; just miles and miles of open land, just us in our little brick home.

I watch Sister sleep, her face as full as the moon. My face has Father's squarish angles I have only seen in pictures. She is small like Mother, who was beautiful when she was young, despite her lame leg. Of course a man from work would like her.

I stroke Sister's hair and watch her quiet breathing. I must have fallen asleep too, because in the blue of dawn, I am still kneeling by her bed and have to tiptoe to my room.

Strangers' voices wake me later in the day; I am frozen to the bed. Sister sounds floaty when she speaks English. In Cantonese, her voice returns to normal: "Mother, this is *Gerald*. He wants to know if he can come over for dinner tonight." Mother agrees. If he is asking for permission, he must be a gentleman.

Then, his voice rings out, happy and eager, but also rough. It washes over me like a dry washcloth, and I let it. When the front door shuts, I rush to my window and there I see him, a real *man*, curly brown hair peeking out of a woollen hat, opening the car door for Sister. She drives off with him. She didn't say goodbye to me.

Saturday is our special day when she and I run errands. She buys groceries or returns library books while I wait in her car. Sometimes I lie flat in the back, so no one can see me and demand to know why I am here. If I get scared and feel like I can't breathe, I think of snow. I remind myself that I wouldn't have known snow if I hadn't come to Canada.

But I still love going with her. It's the only thing we do, just the two of us.

I am looking at the clock again: two hours since she left, five until she comes home with him.

I massage Mother's shoulders as she dozes uselessly in her wheelchair in front of the TV. She must nap every day after lunch. I crawl quietly over to change the channels. Click. A cartoon mouse scampers into his hole. Click. Big men in colourful underwear hit each other with chairs; the audience roars. So many different worlds are at my fingertips. Click.

A lady is wiping away tears. I lower the volume and lean close to her beautiful pale face, blue eyes, and flowing golden hair.

She's in a Canadian kitchen with a gleaming oven and so much space she could dance around without bumping into anything. But she doesn't dance, of course, because she is sad.

Soon I find out why: she discovered that her husband likes another woman very much. And now, he must suffer. She makes his favourite cherry pie, bleeding juice onto her wooden cutting board from where she pierces each halved cherry-heart. She places a bucket marked with a skull on the counter and, with rubber gloves on, sprinkles dark powder from the bucket—

"What filth is this?" Mother is awake. "Naughty girl! You've changed the channels." Mother switches back to Fairchild. "Don't know why women here strut around the kitchen wearing so much jewellery."

I crawl back to Mother's feet, stunned. The dark-haired lady felt so hurt that she could hate someone she once loved. I imagine how she found out: coming back home out of the blue, she would have opened her front door and heard low tones and loud thuds, found clothes in careless piles, furniture overturned, a tangle of hair and legs. It could be a crime scene, if not for the two people—kissing!

On TV, a smiling school girl hands her report card to her grandmother.

Six o'clock, and no one is home. On weekends, we eat at six. Sister knows this. But Sister is still with her friend in the outside world beyond my window.

This cold Saturday leaves nothing interesting to look at. It has been night-dark for hours. I've done the laundry, scrubbed the floors and toilets with brownish Dettol that turns milky in water, cooked dinner even though Sister had said not to.

Watching the barren trees whop in the wind makes me think of the sad lady on TV. *Forget about him,* I want to tell her. *There are other people who care for you.* I'd pat her hand. *You shouldn't be surprised, some — no — most men are horrid, Mother says.* When she stops crying, then, maybe, I'd ask, *What is that powder? Will it kill him?* Also, *What is it like for a man to sink into you?*

The hallway lights snap on! I must have fallen asleep, because two figures have appeared in the hallway: Sister in her creamy parka next to a tall figure. My mind is spinning. He is here. He is inside my house.

"Gerald, come meet my sister," Sister chirps in English.

"Hi," he says, his large hands suddenly around mine. "Priscilla talks about you all the time. I feel like I already know you."

He's holding a bundle of blooming white lilies wrapped in brown paper and finished with a satin bow. He gives Mother the flowers.

"For you, Auntie," he says with a little look to Sister, who nods.

Mother draws her mouth into a tight smile, and I know why. White is the colour of the dead.

As I slip into the kitchen to set the table, Mother grumbles to Sister, "Why didn't you say something to him? Now I have to be polite and put these in water?"

"Is everything okay?" he asks brightly.

"Mother," Sister says, "you want me to tell this nice man, who wanted to get you a gift, who isn't even Chinese, not to buy you flowers?" Sister takes the lilies to the sink.

"Can I help with something?" he asks, looking less cheery.

"If a gentleman cares for a lady, she can make him do anything," says Mother.

"Did you know lilies are good luck in Chinese culture? They represent the coming of sons," he quips. Sister turns and stares. And suddenly I start to giggle. A Canadian *man*, sitting in my kitchen, talking about sons!

"Is something funny?" He chuckles along. "Priscilla?"

"I'm not sure." Sister laughs a little too. I cover my mouth with both hands, but my giggling leaks out in fits. "Maybe you should sit down," Sister says in Cantonese, guiding me to the table.

"No!"

"Oh, be good and let me get dinner."

I trip, scrambling for the seat farthest from him. Sister sets the table, and chatters about their day in a mix of Cantonese and English, asking him to agree or disagree with her report of what they did, to which he always nods, but all I can do is look at his thick hands and try to shush my pounding heart. I must get him out of my house. I want to yell, to banish him, but all my throat can muster are cackles. I start to pant. Mother is staring at me, Sister is staring, *he* is staring.

"I … bathroom!" I run out of the kitchen.

Inside the bathroom, I breathe again. My neck is stiff where I have been hunching, my mind is whirling something crazy. I run the tap and close my eyes and slip into the deep glug of water rushing down the drain. I splash some water on my face. Cool round drops wet my eyelashes like I have been crying. I must get him out of my house.

When I open the door, he is striding down the hall to me, smiling stupidly, miming washing his hands and pointing to the bathroom. I know what I must do.

I grab his sweater and kiss him square on that smiling mouth. He freezes at first. Then, he starts to struggle, his body writhing against me. I'm surprised by my own strength. Maybe he isn't struggling very hard.

"What the hell?" he hisses into my face when he finally pushes me off.

"Did someone yell?" Sister rushes towards us. I go to her, sniffling, and she holds me. "Are you crying?"

"Is this a prank, Priscilla?" He is flailing his arms now. "Is this why you were all laughing? Why would she *do* that?"

Sister searches my face for answers. I don't want her to hurt, but she must know. She will see that I did this for us, to protect us.

I say in English, "We kissed."

"No. No!" he yells, as Sister lets go of me, asking, "What?"

Hot guilt bubbles into my throat. I try to speak, but what more is there to say? Sister's face screws into a mask of horror. I take off up the stairs.

Under my bed, I can hear their loud shrieking below: Sister, him, and Mother, too. They speak over each other, in a confusion of languages, and nothing gets communicated except anger. Then, a door slams. A car grumbles to life. I curl my head closer to my knees. Their ugly noises echo in my ears, my chest is heaving, and the carpet is wet, though I don't remember starting to cry. Only Cantonese shouting now. Sister yells at Mother that it is her fault, and Mother says it can't be true, that I am a good girl. Their voices ring on and on.

I don't know when everything will settle back into how it should be. All I want is to keep the three of us safe and together inside. Sister will understand soon. Then, she will thank me.

For now, I can only weather the storm. Up above it all, I can only hold tight to myself, to the feather feeling of snowflakes on my cheek, to the soft tingle of his mouth on mine.

PRACTISING THE ART OF FORGETTING

Soramimi Hanarejima

Soramimi Hanarejima is the author of *Visits to the* Confabulatorium, *a fanciful story collection that Jack Cheng said "captures moonlight in Ziploc bags and gives us the pleasure of opening them, one by one." Soramimi's recent work can be found in* Fiction Kitchen Berlin, Ninth Letter, Tahoma Literary Review *and* Typehouse. *He has appeared in* Pulp Literature *before, with 'The Theft of Confidence' in Issue 17, Winter 2018.*

$\mathcal{P}$ractising the Art of Forgetting

As soon as we're in the schoolyard for morning recess, we lose no time circling up, cross-legged on the grass — like every Tuesday before forgetting time. Starting with Diandra, we take turns sharing what we've chosen to forget to free up space in our minds for new things. Important things like long division and the meaning of different clouds.

As Diandra explains each of the memories in front of her, I listen closely. I tell her that she's right about that last memory: It is pointless to remember how bored she was at the car dealership on Saturday afternoon.

"I mean, look at how long that memory is," I add, pointing to the sluggish scene glowing on the clover patch by her right knee. "And it's pretty much all the same thing." The memory shows a car dashboard and the view out the windshield while Diandra sat in a showroom model.

"Ugh, yeah," she groans as Lumina nods in agreement.

I don't know what else to say, but there are still plenty of chances to comment on everyone else's memories.

Sure enough, Marzon tells us about his, and I spot another chance to make some remarks.

"I bet you are going to get all these approved right away. Just like Foirene and Cyania do," I say, the moment he is done.

His eyes brighten at the comparison to our classmates. They get full approval so easily, the catchy songs and cartoon episodes they've picked to forget always pleasing Ms Perdont. The rest of us are getting there, though. We've come a long way from bringing in the memories that make us feel bad, and now choose memories that are bad for 'good' reasons.

Barely a month ago, I overheard Marzon protesting, "But memories of the fight make me upset," followed by Ms Perdont saying, "That will make you think twice about fighting in the future, won't it?"

"I guess so," was all he could manage.

But now, Marzon's five memories for this week seem solid. Two are of video games he's been playing. Both just hours of a screen bright with mythological beasts and glittery explosions in colourful fantasy landscapes, minus—he points out—the end of each game. I imagine what he wants to remember: dropping his game controller to the carpet a split second after some nerve-wracking, sword-and-magic combat with the last monster, his cramped hands shooting up over his head in triumph.

"Ms Perdont will definitely like how you're giving up a ton of video game violence," I assure him.

This comment gets Quido to chime in.

"Yeah, and it's cool that you're keeping the best part of playing those games—beating them," he says, impressed.

I grin at Quido's words, at what they mean. Even though he's been excused from forgetting time—his recent growth spurt gave him plenty more space in his mind—Quido still hangs out with us on Tuesday mornings. He still likes finding out the memories we've chosen and why we decided on them. And because of this, he's helping me with my plan without knowing it.

Quido goes on, telling Marzon that he's bound to feel better after forgetting his annoyance at his brother for eating that last brownie. Later, in the middle of Lumina's sharing, Quido says there is definitely no need to remember her parents' most recent argument because it's "so petty"—easily using a word I don't know but feel I should.

Before Lumina gets to share her third memory, the bell rings. I feel a little bad that she was interrupted, but mostly I'm relieved that recess is over before anyone asks about my picks for this week. As we walk toward the school's back entrance, I see Wenderly talking excitedly with Trina and slow my pace to fall behind. I look back at the tennis court, pretending to be interested in the match two college girls are playing.

When Ms Perdont comes over to my desk to look at the memories I have laid out, I'm glowing. This line-up is my strongest yet. Taking a cue from Foirene and Cyania, I have the two game shows I watched while bored last night. Then there's last week's daydream of kissing Trina, totally random and weird—I'd rather have a times table in my memory than this. Finishing things off, I've got a nightmare where I am struggling to restrain a man with big scissors, and lunch last Friday when Wenderly gave everyone at our cafeteria table a lesson on using a swear word I don't like the sound of.

But Ms Perdont doesn't immediately approve these, and my smile fades. She leans over my desk for a closer look at the luminous little scenes. I thought if there were a memory she'd take issue with, it would be the one of Wenderly because even though swearing can be bad, understanding how people express feelings can be good. Instead, it's the daydream about Trina that Ms Perdont peers at, as if searching it for something she's sure is there. Something I've missed.

"Nice work overall," she says. "This one, though."

She points to the memory she's been scrutinizing, and my heart flings up against my ribs.

"What? Why would I need to remember that?" I blurt, surprising myself.

Ms Perdont's eyes widen for a moment.

"All right," she says. "Forget the daydream, then, if you feel strongly about it. But before you do, write about it in your journal. You don't have to show me what you write, but promise me you will write something."

"OK, I promise," I say, and I mean it.

With that, she checks off everything on my record-keeping sheet and also puts a star next to "daydream about Trina." Right away I'm smiling again, not as widely as before but with pride now. I just got my first five out of five! Ms Perdont smiles too, like we share a secret.

My gaze follows Ms Perdont as she walks over to Diandra's desk, going right past Quido's where he's reading a book. Instantly I'm again jealous that he doesn't have to go through forgetting time, but then I'm not so sure that I should be jealous. How would he forget something like my daydream—just ignore it until it fades away? Or get rid of it without any approval from a teacher? My assigned seat in the cafeteria is next to Trina, but it will be easier now that the forgetting is done. I'll ask him during lunch.

MOONS OF SATURN

James Dorr

James Dorr's most recent book, Tombs: A Chronicle of Latter-Day Times of Earth, is a novel-in-stories from Elder Signs Press. He works mostly in dark fantasy / horror with some forays into science fiction and mystery. The Tears of ISIS was a 2013 Stoker Award finalist for Fiction Collection. Other books include Strange Mistresses: Tales of Wonder and Romance, Darker Loves: Tales of Mystery and Regret, and his all-poetry Vamps (A Retrospective). 'The Moons of Saturn' first appeared in Tomorrow magazine in July 1993. An Active Member of SFWA and HWA, Dorr invites readers to visit his blog at jamesdorrwriter.wordpress.com.

Moons of Saturn

Phoebe, with her retrograde motion . . .

We laughed about that when the Voyager photographs were on TV. Her real name *was* Phoebe, named for the mother of the Sun. Or that's what she said.

"You must be Enceladus," she said on a different night, when the news showed the space probe closer to Saturn. Never mind my real name or background. "Enceladus was the most powerful of the storm giants. Savage, yet noble. And, according to the Greek legends, he was born not in the usual way, but from the spilling of his father's blood."

"Shouldn't I be Iapetus instead?" I asked. "The creator of man? Or, more to the point, the moon whose orbit is closest to Phoebe's?"

"No," she said. "Between us, we encompass all the moons" — that was before Mimas's pictures were broadcast — "you next to the brooding bulk of Saturn, the god-devourer of his children, and me the outermost moon of them all."

"And you with your retrograde motion," I said. "Widdershins to the others' orbits."

Discovered in 1898, the TV continued, flashing back to the Voyager pictures. *Phoebe circles more than eight million miles from Saturn, one of only two of the moons with its orbital plane tilted at an angle to that of the rings . . .*

"Another difference. Another out-of-stepness," I said.

We laughed again, Phoebe and I. Phoebe, with her passion for ancient legends and myths. Her fascination was not so much with science as with the fantasies that could be spun from it.

As for me, as I say, never mind my name or my background. You may have known me. Suffice it to say that I had money willed to me by an aunt, enough that I needn't work unless it held my interest. That I had had a good education.

That Phoebe and I loved each other deeply.

Discovered in 1789, the TV news said. This was for Mimas.

"The year of the guillotine," Phoebe broke in, as if the announcer were talking to her. "Of revolution and blood in France."

"Shhhh," I said as the voice went on. *. . . discovered the same year as Enceladus.* There was a shift as a picture of *my* moon formed on the TV so they could be compared. *Mimas orbits less than 120,000 miles from its parent, while Enceladus, the next moon out . . .*

"No," Phoebe said. "Saturn was *never* our father. You, Mimas, the storm giants, and I were all born of Gaea and Uranus. Saturn, too, was a son of Uranus."

"I know, Phoebe," I whispered. I kissed her.

"Wait," she said. "Before, I'd forgotten Mimas, the innermost moon. The one of our siblings who freed Earth's volcanoes. And now they say there are other, tiny moons even closer to Saturn than he is. But last night I had a dream about Mimas. And you and me. The two of you are bound together—discovered the same year—and thus, somehow, Mimas is bound to me also."

"I heard you scream last night," I said. "While you were sleeping. It was only once, so I didn't wake you."

"I haven't been feeling well," she said. "It's probably nothing."

I kissed her again, harder this time, and she kissed me back. That night we made love in front of the TV while Voyager's arc swung it closer to Saturn. We watched, in each other's arms, as the pictures formed on the screen.

Saturn. In some cultures, it's called the 'Death Planet'. Phoebe started, then kissed me quickly. *To astrologers, it's said to be the ruler of Capricorn, lord of winter. Saturn was known from ancient times . . .*

We watched. An orange globe appeared, strikingly oblate.

. . . with a diameter 9.4 times that of Earth, and yet a day on Saturn's surface lasts less than eleven hours here on Earth . . .

"That explains the flattened poles," I said. "That fast a rotation. Centrifugal forces would — "

"Maybe," she said. "But look at those swollen stripes and patterns. It moves *too* fast. And see. Enceladus, think of what it would look like from your orbit. From my moon, it seems like just a jewel in the sky, but from where you are, it must be enormous."

I tried to imagine it filling my vision. Rising over a rock-strewn plain, over so huge an arc it looked as though it must crush, of necessity, any object that dared stand beneath it. But then the TV picture pulled back.

. . . the rings . . .

Phoebe gasped. We hugged each other.

. . . believed by some scientists to have once been an asteroid sucked, vampire-like, from its proper orbit when it came too close. In time, gravitational forces destroyed it . . .

I stood again on Enceladus's surface, seeing the rings now shoot from the huge disk like two immense arrows. In my mind,

I saw them on edge, because only Phoebe and Iapetus have orbits that deviate from the rings' plane to any appreciable degree. Here, though, the space probe approached from an angle, slightly below, as it wove its complex path around Saturn …

… what scientists call Cassini's Division, forming a wide gap between what we now call the A Ring and B Ring. But look. Now we can see there are more. A C Ring, possibly D and E rings. And outside the A Ring, a narrower pattern is coming into focus. It isn't smooth-looking like the rings we've seen but looks almost as though it were made from two long, separate strands and braided …

I laughed out loud. Phoebe had braided her hair that evening. I nuzzled the back of her neck and kissed her. She didn't respond.

"Phoebe?" I whispered.

I saw she was sleeping.

I carried her up to bed that night, and the following night too. Then, at her request, I made her a new bed—a sort of nest—on the living room floor in front of the TV. I went out during the day and left her watching the pictures, then joined her afterward to watch the news and the evening specials.

Sometimes the pictures we'd see would be new ones broadcast by Voyager as we sat, arms around each other. More often they'd be ones received already—that she'd seen already—but half the time she couldn't remember.

And sometimes she'd say she *did* remember a picture being sent for the first time.

"Perhaps it was in a dream," she would say. "Or something I read. I just thought I saw it."

I worried about her.

On the third day, I called a doctor to come and see her. She protested—"I just feel faint sometimes"—but I insisted. He gave her a thorough examination but found nothing wrong. He gave her a tonic.

He thought that she might use a bit more fresh air.

She laughed when he left us. "You know I prefer the indoors," she said. "I just—I don't know. Since I was a girl, I've always enjoyed the feeling of waking while still in a dream. I just feel more tired now."

She took her tonic. I tried it, too, at her insistence, at night when we watched the Voyager probe start its long ascent back through the moons of Saturn: Mimas, a ball of ice from what the scientists said on TV. Enceladus, my moon, mostly ice too, scarcely more than 30,000 miles farther out than the orbit of Mimas.

"I dreamed of you and Mimas again last night," she said. "How you—and I, too—are bound together. I dreamed of Rhea, its mineral surface sparkling with jewels."

Rhea was still just a dot in the distance on the TV. Yet Phoebe went on.

"I dreamed of the mining colony there. Oh, maybe not right now, but in the future they'll go there for gemstones. You'll see, Enceladus."

I almost *could* see it when I closed my eyes. The pressure domes. The space-suited men digging into the rock. But then, when I opened my eyes again and gazed at Phoebe, I saw she was paler.

I called a new doctor. We lived on a back road outside the city, and soon there was a succession of doctors plying their way across the countryside to our home. They gave her tests of various sorts, but none could find anything wrong with Phoebe, at least not physically. Some prescribed pills.

On my way back from work—oh yes, I still worked then. Never mind what I did. But one afternoon, on my way home,

I drove through a different part of the city than I usually went through. On an impulse, I stopped and got out of my car.

I'd already stopped once before at a drugstore for Phoebe's pills, although I was convinced they were doing her no good. But now, as I looked at the stores around me, I had an odd feeling of having once stood in this very same part of the city before. It couldn't be true, unless it had been years ago — it was near the city university, in what once had been a residential student section but since had degraded to one of those over-the-hill hippie neighbourhoods rife with herbalists and tarot readers, 'new age' gear and shops advertising magic stones and 'pyramid power'. And yet I *knew* when I turned the corner, I'd find still another doctor for Phoebe.

His sign was a three-by-five index card pasted onto a door frame. I knew where to find it. I knew I *would* find it.

It said Dr Mimas.

I raced up the stairs to a dingy hallway and, without looking, I knew to open the door to my left. Inside was an elderly, tired-looking man, his beard — somehow I knew it once had been fire red — the colour of old, much-trampled snow.

I explained my problem. About Phoebe's sickness. He asked to know more, and I told him about how we watched together as Voyager's pictures formed on the TV. He held up his hand then.

"You are Enceladus?" he asked.

I nodded, startled. "I haven't told you my name yet," I blurted.

"Perhaps I guessed it," he said. "Or perhaps I had reason to expect you. We are like brothers, you and I, although maybe not in the usual blood way." He handed me a dust-covered bottle, about the size of a whisky bottle, and then he smiled up at me. "I once knew Phoebe."

"What is this?" I asked.

"Another tonic for Phoebe," he said, his face again serious. "It's artemisia — oil of wormwood. As a tincture, it's sometimes called absinthe. In its true form it's not exactly legal these days, but it won't do her harm and, if you try it with her, it may help you to relax as well."

I looked at it dubiously. "How much?" I asked. He named a price that seemed surprisingly low and told me to come back if Phoebe got worse. I paid him and left and, when I got home, Phoebe and I tried a spoonful together.

It seemed to perk her up a little, at least for a while. I turned on the TV, and we watched together as pictures of Tethys, then Dione, appeared.

. . . both discovered by Cassini in 1684, nine years after his observation that Saturn's rings were divided in two. And now we have proof there's a second moon in Dione's orbit, a 'Dione B' that circles the planet sixty degrees ahead of its namesake. Cassini had already discovered the moons Iapetus and Rhea . . .

"I had a dream while you were away," Phoebe said when the announcer had finished. "It was about the stone of Rhea. Once, when the universe was young, some fell to Earth. It fell on the hillside, in the forest behind where we live now . . ."

"Yes?" I prompted, when she became silent.

"A moment," she said. She closed her eyes. "I dreamed of a cabin, built in the woods." Her voice was chantlike. "A steepled roof, with openings to let light in . . ."

She fell silent again, and I saw she was sleeping. Quietly, I put on my shoes and crept out of the house and into the forest. I climbed the hillside. The sun had set, but in the moonlight I saw, near the top, a jumble of stone that cropped out through the underbrush. Some of it sparkled — gneiss, most likely, yet in the pale light it flashed, multicoloured, as if it were studded with precious jewels.

That night, I dreamed of Phoebe's cabin too.

In spite of the absinthe, Phoebe's condition worsened nightly. I called more doctors, many whose theories lay in less-than-traditional medicines, yet, like the others, all were baffled. I sought out Dr Mimas again and told him, were she to die, I wished to die too. But all he would tell me was "share *everything* with your love, Enceladus. Share in her dreams that you may both be free."

I thought, then, of the cabin we dreamed of. I quit my work and had plans drawn up. I hired men to build it.

During the days, I supervised the cabin's construction to make sure all details were done right. I had the men work fast — within a day, the first of the massive rock walls was standing and, by the week's end, the jewelled peak of its pyramid-shaped roof was set in its place. Although I was unused to physical labour, I did this last with my very own hands. I had not exaggerated when I told Dr Mimas that, if Phoebe would die, I wished to die with her.

And throughout all this frantic activity, Voyager continued its measured path out through the moons.

Tethys, the Diones, all fell behind in the wake of the space probe. Phoebe — *my* Phoebe — slept most of the day now, waking only for the nightly reports on its progress. A sparkling jewel appeared on the TV — another ice moon, the announcer said.

But this was Rhea.

Phoebe started, visibly shaken.

"Hush," I told her. "I've built your cabin, just as we dreamed it." I gave her her tonic, and took some with her, a half cup for each of us. "I've had it built in the woods, like we saw it within our minds. The tall, pointed arches, the peak of the roof, the cut stone of the floor. I've put in a couch for you so, if you wish to, you can lie out there …"

She half-rose to kiss me, to show her thanks, and I sat by her side as the pictures continued.

Next on Voyager's journey, the TV said, *we'll come to Titan, discovered in 1655 by the Dutch astronomer Huygens …*

"Titan," she whispered. "The namesake of all of us. The first discovered."

"Yes," I whispered back. "But *this* is Rhea. See. On the screen now. The cratered surface …"

So the nights went on. Titan now filled Voyager's sky while Phoebe dozed fitfully in my arms. I half-dreamed with her, seeing not just the globe on the screen but its surface as well—its methane fountains vaporizing in orange haze, filling the air, its sparkling liquid nitrogen pools, its view of Saturn, peeking through clouds like the moon of our own Earth seen after a storm.

And still she worsened. She didn't even wake when Hyperion filled the screen. Two-faced Iapetus, black rock on one side and ice on the other, passed silently too, with Phoebe only stirring slightly. Then Phoebe, the moon—my Phoebe's namesake—appeared, a glowing red point on the screen.

My Phoebe half-opened one of her eyes. I gazed at her lips as she tried to part them.

"See," I whispered. I shouldn't have said it, but seeing her paleness next to the image drove the words from my lips. "See," I told her. "Even your moon has more colour than you do."

"No!" she screamed. "All I see is blood colour."

She sat bolt upright.

I tried to calm her. Held her close to me. Shared her medicine — a half cup for each of us — just as before when she'd started at the passing of Rhea.

"It's all right," I told her. I kissed her cheek, startled myself at its coldness.

"No," she said again. "Look at the blood."

I closed my eyes, trying to imagine, but saw only darkness.

"Again, Enceladus. Let your mind reach out. Turn where you're standing and look behind you."

I did so. I felt her standing beside me. I turned as she did and suddenly saw the sky fill with redness.

"What is it?" I whispered.

"Disaster," she said. "The miners of Rhea. A meteorite has struck their colony, breaking its dome. The air is rushing in …"

"Out," I corrected. "Rhea is airless. They said on the TV …"

"They lied, Enceladus. Don't you see? The miners are there *now*, not just in the future. But the air of Rhea is poison."

"What can we do, then?" I felt her push from me. Felt more than saw her fade into the distance.

"I am bound with Rhea. We both are. Not just with Rhea, but all of the moons, and all who live on them. But I cannot help them — I'm too weak already. You must go to Titan …"

I strained to listen as her voice faded then came back again, like a radio signal in the far distance.

"… must journey to the surface of Titan without me, Enceladus. There is a wizard who has a serum. A brilliant alchemist. Only with that can you save the miners. Only with that can you save my life with theirs …"

I no longer heard her. Instead I heard a ringing of chimes and a rushing of winds. I opened my eyes and saw I was hurtling through orange clouds, my ship's rockets blazing.

Below me was rock. Rock, and nitrogen pools, and fountains.

I knew, somehow, where the ship's controls were, and I steered to a landing.

I disembarked. I felt the wind whistling around my spacesuit, wondering how I could hear through its plastic-coated metal. I strode through jagged, red-coloured mountains, across yellow plains. I swam frozen, brilliant-blue rivers — I don't know how, in my heavy clothing. Suffice that I did it.

I saw the animals: dinosaur-like, green-scaled creatures that munched on crystal.

I came to a cave.

I threaded my way between two huge boulders and descended a twisting passage, my way lit by a red-orange glow. I came to a vast, level-floored hollow, domed over with purple and brown and gray rock. And I saw, his back to me, a giant clothed in robes as black as the empty space Saturn and its moons whirled through.

I wondered what to say. Then words came to me and, even though my faceplate was closed, I heard my voice echo as if in challenge.

"I am Enceladus, he who was born of his father's lost blood. I seek the wizard" — I knew his name now! — "the wizard Iapetus, maker of humankind."

"Then you seek your own brother," the figure said, turning slowly. I realized as he said the words that I was a giant too. "You come to save Phoebe, our mutual sister, but you are too late. The serum is used up."

"No!" I shouted. I stopped as Iapetus pushed back his hood. I gazed at a face as double-sided as the moon that bore his name, one half the white of the purest snow and the other dead black—the black of his clothing.

"No," I said again, now in a whisper. "I come for the miners. The serum is for them. Through *them* I'll save Phoebe."

Iapetus laughed. "Don't you see, my brother, that in my power is both death *and* life? I am the father of Prometheus, bringer of fire. The father of Atlas, who holds up the sky. The father of man, yes. But, just as I preside at birth, the death of all mankind is also mine to withhold or bestow."

"I understand only that I need the serum." I lunged at Iapetus, striking with both fists. I forced him backward.

Iapetus raised his own hands to defend himself. "Wait, my brother. You don't understand yet. Don't you know that death is needed—for in death is new life?"

I found myself armed now with sword and shield, while my adversary counterattacked with net and trident. The net of his words. I found myself tangled, then, with a shout, I shook them from me.

"If I must destroy you, so be it, Iapetus. I *will* have the serum. Or, if I cannot and Phoebe is doomed, then you must kill me too."

I rushed at Iapetus, striking blindly, pushing him backward once again. Without his net he was helpless before me. I lunged. I twisted. I opened his chest, his shoulder, his belly. I laughed in my triumph.

But still he struck back at me—one final blow.

"You don't understand yet. She's dead already."

I felt the trident's points tear the inner part of my thigh.

I felt myself falling.

I heard my brother's voice, far away. "It is not for you to attack *me*, Enceladus. For that I curse you. That you will recover. That you, the strongest of all my brothers, are doomed to live on …"

I woke to the memory of clashing chimes. To a rushing of air. I woke at Phoebe's side, clutching her coldness within my arms. I, the youngest of the sons of Uranus and Gaea, formed when my father's life splashed onto the ground of my mother.

I knew what I must do.

Slowly, painfully, feeling my wound stiffen with each step, I carried her body out into the woods, to the cabin I'd built. I laid her gently on the couch I had furnished it with when I'd still hoped she might use it in her recovery.

I loosened her clothing then kissed her softly.

The following morning I went to the city.

I sought Dr Mimas, but, when I arrived at the building where his office should be, I found it boarded up. It didn't matter. I knew, if I looked, I could find a new source of absinthe elsewhere.

More important, I searched out a slaughterhouse that would sell me cows' blood and ask no questions. That became *my* new tonic. I found a medical supplier who sold me catheters and needles, tube arms, pressure bulbs and bottles. I bought a second recovery couch to set next to Phoebe's.

I knew our blood types matched. We had been tested some years in the past. And I had had a good education, including a smattering of medical knowledge.

Enough to do what I knew I had to.

That evening I began the first of Phoebe's transfusions. Her pulse, when I felt it, was still nonexistent, but now, at least, when I looked at her cheeks I saw traces of colour. When the transfusion was done, we made love, my stroking as gentle as it had been the first time we'd done so.

Of course she didn't respond that night, or the next, or the next. But still, every evening, I gave her my blood, mixed with a tablespoon of absinthe bled into the catheter. Every morning, I renewed my own strength with the blood from the slaughterhouse. Blood and absinthe—Dr Mimas' tonic. Semen. Life fluid. Just as my father had granted to me. At least her disease was now in remission.

And every evening, winter or summer, I opened the louvers in the roof of our pyramid cabin to show her the stars. I took to reading ephemerides so I could point out the position of Saturn.

In the fourth year, I built a telescope with a mirror so we could watch the moons together during our lovemaking. I was happy enough her condition was stable.

Oh, you wouldn't know me if you were to see me on the street now, even though we might once have been the best of friends. The nights, the transfusions, the love take their toll.

I've paled, and I've lost weight. My skin peels in sunlight. The blood from the slaughterhouse—I need more and more now—I scarcely eat otherwise—brings me less strength now than when I first started.

My wound, after all this time, has not yet healed.

But Phoebe, ah, Phoebe …

Phoebe, of late, has shown signs of improvement.

HOAX

Susan Pieters

Susan writes from the mysterious depths of East Vancouver. This was an Hour Story written with Jen and Mel from an idea given to her by Ed Levinson. Apparently his wife, writer Cathy Levinson, refuses to spin his stories for him. Wise woman.

Hoax

Ed was just a guy in the wrong job at the wrong time. When he got the word that he was fired, he questioned it, as he questioned everything.

"The Internet," he was told, "is being shut down with the exception of essential services. Like medical stuff. No more banking, investments."

Ed scoffed. He knew the real reason. They were leaking money faster than a fibre optic cable could break apart.

"What about Netflix?" Ed asked.

"Essential service," they replied. Deadpan. Without blinking.

He took his revenge in the middle of the night. In a world gone crazy, he lifted a photo of an army recruit with a shaved head and face, and made the post. "Army discovers bald men have higher resistance to COVID-19."

He sourced the story through the usual anonymous channels: Instagram and Facebook sites that were no longer monitored properly due to the outbreak.

He laughed when, no pun intended, the story went viral.

Men started shaving their heads. Gone were the big beards

and lumberjack shirts. They were replaced with stark skinhead shines and smooth baby-bottom faces.

The women started as well. Gone were all the long locks of hair. Scarves became popular, and tied-up bandanas, as if there had been a wave of chemotherapy patients.

People really believed him. Ed started to feel bad. So many shorn heads. Barbershops reopened as an essential service and had line-ups of people, spaced six feet apart, waiting to shed their hair.

The at-home cuts were more noticeable and less even, but the patchy spotted-skull look became a trend. It became #patriotcut on Twitter, and photo threads exploded on Instagram. Medical doctors on YouTube encouraged haircuts as a sanitary antivirus measure.

Ed couldn't believe no one had tested this idea and reviled it publicly. He couldn't believe people were fearful enough to embrace such a drastic action without proof. He realized how much people wanted to do something—anything—to stop the pandemic.

Then the last irony occurred.

The pandemic started to subside. Contagion was down. The curve was flattening further and faster. Scientists traced the drop to the date people started shaving their heads.

Ed, through the FBI, was discovered. Found out. Called in for questioning. Called to report to Washington, virtually.

It was the moment of truth. They were onto him.

Ed looked in his bathroom mirror. He took out his own razor, shook his head, and started to shave off the beard he had maintained for twenty years. If he didn't, and they saw him on Zoom, they would know he had spread fake news.

He asked his wife to shave his head.

She obliged.

Ed appeared on the Zoom platform, appropriately shorn and ready for questions. He was prepared to lie through his teeth to excuse himself from prosecution.

"How did you know?" was the first question.

"I looked up historical figures from the Black Death, and found that monks with bald and shorn pates and no beards survived the pandemic at a higher rate."

"And the military men surviving better?"

"I, uh, can't reveal my sources," Ed said. "But it's common sense that masks work better without beards."

The FBI agents looked at each other on their super-secure Zoom channel.

"We aren't going to look further into this," they said. "But we want to tell you that our scientists have concluded you were right. Germs captured on hair live longer and spread contagion faster. We want to offer you our thanks. Personally."

The screen switched to another man, hardly recognizable except for the orange skin and the pale circles around his tanning-bed eyes. Gone was the comb-over, the eyebrows, even the nose hair. "Ed, it's tremendous. You've saved lives. I owe you my thanks. You're a hero. We're going to call this the Ed Cure in your honour."

Ed put his hand to his mouth to hide his emotion. He was glad he had saved lives with his bit of fake news. But his real reward?

"Seeing you like this, Mr President," Ed said, "is reward enough."

STARRY NIGHTS

David Milne

David Milne was born in northern BC and now lives in Calgary with his wife, Lindsay, and daughter, Paige. His fiction has previously appeared in Geist, Grain, and Qwerty.

Starry Nights

Phillip wakes in the silence of an unfamiliar room, confused about where he is. The soft glow of a streetlight comes through the window, painting the walls in blue and silver. The ceiling is covered with glow-in-the-dark star stickers which, while weak with age, still faintly shine.

He sits up on a bare mattress, his sleeping bag unzipped in the heat and falling aside. He turns on a lamp that sits on the empty nightstand. The walls are bare, the carpet marked with prints of absent furniture.

From the street, Phillip is a thin silhouette illuminated in the blazing white glow of a window suspended in a wall of night. The silhouette stands, thin and worried and drawing back from something.

Phillip goes to the window, glances out, and pulls the drapes closed. He gets back into the sleeping bag, looks around once more, and turns out the light.

In the morning, Phillip eats a bowl of cereal at the kitchen table, sun lancing through narrow windows. The old panes bend and warp the light, creating shadows where there should be none, twisting the sunlight into bulbous shapes. Phillip doesn't seem to notice. His shirt says, *The White Whale Is <u>Right</u> Behind You.*

There are piles of fresh cardboard boxes in the corner beside the table, folded flat and sitting in stacks. The smell of them makes Phillip think of moving — the rented vans and long stairs in buildings with no elevators, the sense of being unmoored and loose in the world, the excitement and anxiety.

A convincing simulation of a service bell dings from his phone. Phillip spins it around to face him, taps the screen, and stares.

The message: "How's it going there? You up?"

He types with one finger, a tiny lemon twist in his lips: "Busy packing."

Ding: "I showed Mom the pic of you on the front porch. Since when can you grow a beard?"

Phillip rolls his eyes and swallows Froot Loops bought at a convenience store the previous night. He types: "I've had it forever."

Ding: "We think you should shave it."

He finishes his cereal, wipes milk from his lips, and surveys the cluttered kitchen.

Ding: "Do you have a plan? Have you got a storage place?"

Phillip pokes at the screen. Before he can finish his response, the chime comes again.

Ding: "Do you know how to get to the dump?"

"Oh for fuck," he says. He erases what he's written and types "Go away." Jabs *send* with a missile-like forefinger.

Ding: "Here are directions to it. Closes at 5 so don't waste time :)!"

Phillip ignores the link and pushes the phone away. He gets up and throws his bowl in the sink, where it shatters into a bear-shaped constellation of white ceramic fragments.

In sweat and honest labour, Phillip misplaces the day.

Phillip wakes to the sound of a long, slow creak from the floor above him. He lies still, half-awake and unsure of his surroundings. Street light filters in through blue gauze drapes. The adhesive stars gleam faintly as if from a great distance.

There is another long creak, as if someone had taken a careful step. Phillip's stomach twists, and his eyes leap to the ceiling. Something small and hard bounces on the floor above.

He slides out of bed, tiptoes to the door, opens it, and peers into the hallway. A nightlight in the shape of an old wood stove illuminates the ancient green carpet and the bottom of the wall. Its light can't reach far, dissipating about four steps up the stairs at the end of the hall. He looks back at the bedroom, searching fruitlessly for something blunt.

At the bottom of the stair he finds the light switch that turns on the third-floor light, and he flicks it on.

The ceiling light glaring on the white walls hurts his eyes. The empty stairway is only slightly less daunting than the darkness had been.

He pauses, then climbs the stairs, fists raised, the old wood creaking, and reaches the short upper hallway. The open doors of a bathroom and two small bedrooms await, all dark.

Phillip turns the light on in each room. One bedroom is empty except for stacked boxes, another contains a lone dresser and a bed frame without a mattress. The bathroom is already bare of possessions.

Once every light is on, he exhales and checks the windows. All of them are closed. The corners of his mouth pull down.

He retreats, leaving the third-floor lights ablaze, scouts out the ground floor, and then goes back to his temporary bedroom on the second where, after a quick look back at the hallway, he closes the door. Phillip pulls the drapes open, letting light from the lamppost outside brighten the room. He climbs into bed, stares at the glowing stars, then sleeps.

The afternoon sun pours down through the leaves of tall elms, warming Phillip as he sits on the porch steps, the white paint peeling and chipping away from the grey wood beneath him. The lawn is pristine and short, although Phillip doesn't know who would have cut it. He sits on the stairs, luxuriating in the heat, a fresh beer breathing the summer air beside him.

He holds his phone in both hands. On the screen, a text reads, "How's it going?"

His right index finger carefully picks out letters. "Slowly. She had a lot of stuff."

A pause. Ding: "You're not throwing it all out, are you?"

One finger taps out the letters. "Some to dump. Sellable stuff to storage."

He takes a drink, tastes honest labour.

Ding: "Have you posted anything on Kijiji yet?"

He gives his phone the finger, then types, "How's Mom doing?"

Ding: "She's OK. She's being British about it."

Typing: "Big surprise."

Ding: "We're watching a lot of movies."

Typing: "Tell her I'll call her tonight."

Ding: "Sure …"

"Fuck off," he says, and clicks the phone off.

He sleeps with the drapes closed, a copy of *Hard-Boiled Wonderland* lying open on the mattress beside him. A muffled thump some-where in the house makes him stir but not waken. Then the long, slow creak comes from directly above and his eyes open.

The stars glow overhead, and he is dismayed to find himself here again, hours from dawn and the boundary of daytime possibility. The ceiling groans and he tenses, ready to leap. Something falls, bounces once, and Phillip inhales sharply, holds it, then blows it out loudly.

Phillip climbs out of bed and walks to the door. He grasps the knob and turns it slowly; his free hand is braced against the door as if something might try to fling it wide. He turns the knob all the way and then, still holding a palm against it, gently opens the door.

The hall is in shadow, the nightlight weak. He stands in the doorway, looking right towards the third floor, then left to the stairs down to the main. Phillip studies the unhappy reality of the dark stairway and his obligation to explore it again. Then he shuts the door, turns the bedside lamp on, and pulls the sleeping bag over his head.

Ding: "Almost done?"

Phillip stops loading clothes into a cardboard box and types, "No. Come help."

A minute more of packing and then, ding: "Would love to be there." Ding: "Is crazy here. Contracts need to get signed or we may be packing up this house, too."

Phillip rolls his eyes and slowly types, "You always freak out then get another raise." He hits *send*, stares at the screen.

When there is no sign of a reply, he types again: "They'll give you days off. They love you." He remains hunched over the phone, waiting.

Ding: "Someone needs to be here for Mom."

Typing: "They weren't even close."

Ding: "You don't know how to read her."

He tosses the phone into a corner of the room and starts shovelling clothes into a box, no longer bothering to fold them.

Phillip reads for a long time, the lamp on, his eyes sore and tired, the unzipped sleeping bag just a little too warm. He eventually turns off the lamp. The drapes are closed, but the hall light shines crisply under the door. He keeps the sleeping bag pulled up to just below his eyes — and sweats.

At some point he wakes from a sleep he didn't know had arrived, the stars glowing on the ceiling. The creaking begins. It seems deliberate. Provocative.

He stays where he is, watching the night sky that adheres to the ceiling. The creaking comes again, and then the bang and bounce. Phillip's eyes dart between the ceiling and his bedroom door.

The stars glow softly. Faint bars of streetlight reach through the thin drapes and stand immobile on the wall. The room brightens and darkens intermittently which, Phillip decides, must be the passing of clouds over the moon. An impatient thump comes from above. Phillip's stomach pitches up into his throat, and his body goes rigid. He extends one arm out from the safety of the sleeping bag and turns on the lamp, attempting to restore order and reason. He imagines the unlit bedroom directly above him.

Something slides or is dragged, ending in another dull thump. There is a tap on his door.

It is a single, sharp tap, made with something hard. Phillip sucks air in and sits up, his right hand in a fist.

He stares at the door, fist cocked. There is only silence. Eventually, having filled his head with rationalizations, Phillip props up his un-cased pillow, retrieves his book from the foot of the bed, and reads. Despite the bumps and bangs from above, Phillip continues to read. After the sky turns pale and day starts to fill the room, he falls asleep with the light on.

In the morning, Phillip gets out of bed and goes straight to the third-floor bedroom, where he finds that a small box of trinkets, which he had piled on top of a larger box of clothes, has toppled over. Small framed photos, earrings, and curious glass balls containing blobs of colour are scattered on the carpeted floor.

Phillip stares at the debris. He shovels the items back into the box then hauls the boxes downstairs and piles them outside on the front porch. He slides the empty dresser down the two flights, barely keeping its descent in check, then disassembles the bed frame and carries it down as well. He does all of this without resting, without even bothering to put his shirt on. Then, once the top floor is stripped bare, he eats cereal at the kitchen table, the Froot Loops so sugary that they make him nauseated.

After breakfast and a shower, he loads the contents of the porch into the back of his truck.

Ding: "Almost done? :)"

Typing: "No. Send Dale. I'll buy beer."

Ding: "Everyone here works."

Ding: "You're a single guy with a truck. You chose this life :)"

Ding: "You're going to have it ready for Friday, right?"

Typing: "This is a lot of stuff." He hits *send* and stares at the screen.

Ding: "You're going to be ready for Friday, right???"

Phillip says something under his breath that involves the word 'fuck' but isn't limited to it.

Ding: "Do you want to try and get Mom to talk about it?"

He types aggressively, with a single finger. "She doesn't need to talk. She's an oak."

Ding: "That's what you think. Do your part, OK?"

He shoves a stiff middle finger in front of the screen, his face rictusing. He pulls his arm back, arced to throw the phone, but slows down, calms himself. He sits with his arms on his knees, the phone hanging limp in his right hand.

Typing: "Maybe Mom wants to come out. See if there's stuff she wants to keep."

Ding: "You're inviting Mom?"

Typing: "Sure."

Ding: "She says the past is an anchor and she's too old to carry it."

Typing: "She said that?"

Ding: "Sure did. British."

He stares at the screen for at least half a minute, then drives to the dump, where he hurls old objects into the still air.

At eight, Phillip, tired and crusted in dried sweat, pulls into a mostly empty McDonalds. As he carries his tray to the table, he notices that his hands are shaking and realizes he hasn't eaten since breakfast.

He inhales a two-cheeseburger meal then goes back to the counter and orders McNuggets and a sundae. After he finishes, he sits, slowly sipping a Coke and watching cars go by in the street. He finishes his drink, pulls the lid off, and crunches the ice one cube at a time. With the straw he vacuums the last droplets of liquid out of the empty cup, stares into it, then takes his tray to the garbage. Already he feels heavy and ill.

When Phillip pulls up in front of the house, all the lights are on, revealing the stark, bare walls inside. The emptiness only makes it feel more alien. He sits in the truck.

Typing: "All ready for tomorrow."

He stares at the screen, hoping for contact; the house watches over him. The screen fades and then goes dark.

The ground floor is empty, and he considers sleeping in the living room. The wide open spaces and barren walls, though, are just too much, so he goes upstairs. The mattress is gone now, and his sleeping bag is stretched out on the floor with his book, pillow, and gym bag of clothes. Phillip shuts the door and stands at the window, watching the street. No one goes by. He checks his phone again but has no messages.

He gets into the sleeping bag, skin salty from the long day, and lies there, reading under the inhospitable ceiling light. After half an hour he puts the book down, pulls the sleeping bag over his head, and waits for sleep.

The creaking begins, then a thump. Phillip lies still, keeps his head under the cover. He knows there is nothing left to fall over. He wills himself to sleep.

Something bangs overhead and vibrates the floor beneath him. Phillip bolts upright and stares at the ceiling.

He breathes hard, his teeth bared, chest rising and falling. There is the small, strange noise, like a marble falling onto a wooden floor and rolling — though the room above is carpeted.

"Fuck," he says, and stands up. He pauses at the bedroom door, then yanks it open and steps into the hall, head whipping side to side. He's left all the lights on. Everything is garishly lit, the ceiling lights sterile on the bare walls. Phillip stomps up the stairs. He glares into the bathroom and the smaller bedroom as he passes, confirms they are empty, then reaches the master bedroom at the end of the hall and marches in.

"What the fuck?" he yells, then slams his fist sideways against the wall. "Fuck. What is all the fucking noise about?" He glares around, eyes wide and face unloving. "Is it you, Grandma? I mean, what the fuck? It's me, Phillip. I'm here helping." He looks around. "I'm not taking your stuff, you know? I don't even want to be here. Mom asked me to come." He pauses. "Jesus, you know you're dead, right? You know that it's probably too late to start trying to communicate now."

Phillip's arms wave wildly at his sides. "It's too late," he yells, "to break the fucking family tradition." His eyes boil the empty air, undetectable currents heating and stirring. "What do you want? Knocking shit over and banging on walls isn't getting you anywhere, because I have no idea what your fucking problem is. If you've got something to say …" He waves his hands in the air, uncertain. "Write it in the steam on the bathroom mirror. Fuck."

He stands in his underwear, a bead of sweat rippling through his modest beard, his shoulders pulled back and thin chest thrust forward. Silence.

Phillip goes back downstairs, slams the bedroom door and brushes sweat from his face. He climbs into the sleeping bag, pulls it over his head to shield his eyes from the ceiling light, and falls asleep.

When he wakes the room is dark.

The stars glow on the ceiling. Phillip tries to remember if he turned the light off. Maybe he got up and went to the bathroom and turned it off when he came back? He looks for the bar of hallway light from under the door, and there is none. He blinks several times, gets up, and walks to the door in his underwear, moving slowly and calmly while his heart thumps. He finds the light switch and flips it.

Nothing happens.

He toggles it back and forth, breathing heavily but trying to look calm, as if someone might be watching.

He crouches to pick his phone off the floor and hits the home button. There is no response, no faint haptic vibration. He holds the power button, but nothing happens.

The familiar creak comes from upstairs, followed by a sharp bang that makes Phillip look up, his crouch unsteady. The darkness churns with tiny lights. The stars are falling, are falling from the ceiling, are raining down, still glowing. They lightly touch his hair, tickle his bare arms and back, goosebumps exploding on his skin.

The stars settle gently on the floor, scattered around the room. Thump. Pause. Thump. Phillip stares at the ceiling. Bang. He feels the vibrations in his feet.

The sound is getting louder, the vibration stronger. It seems to be moving towards the stairs.

Phillip looks at the door, stares at the knob with terrible anticipation.

He lunges forward and jerks the door open, like tearing off a Band-Aid, then freezes, staring at the darkness. He leans out, looks to the right, but the blackness is too perfect. Even the wood-stove nightlight is out. To his left are the stairs down to the main floor. From his right comes a terrible, crashing thump, so loud it resonates right through him. It feels like being inside a beating heart. He jumps back, throwing the door closed. There is a bang from the third-floor stairs.

Phillip lurches to the window, tears the drapes aside, and heaves the glass up, the air cool. He turns back abruptly, takes two rapid steps, and grabs his bag off the floor. There is a terrific thump in the hall, and the door swings lazily open. Phillip searches the vacuum beyond. His legs go to rubber.

Phillip runs to the window and dives out onto the slanted porch roof, the angle sending him rolling. The rough asphalt shingles tear at his skin; the air roars as he falls. The terrific, dull force of hitting the lawn shoulder first, sprays stars before his eyes. His bag is lying a dozen feet away, and he scoops it up as he runs for the truck. The street is deserted.

The gentle morning sun finds Phillip sitting on the curb, unshowered and hair akimbo, but fully dressed. The house is silent behind him.

Typing: "Realtor's doing the inspection now. Listing on Monday."

He gently rubs his neck and grimaces. A white panel van passes in the street.

Ding: "Good job, Bro!"

Phillip watches the road and feels a sort of satisfaction. A sense of completion.

Ding: "Are we making a mistake? Maybe we should keep it as a rental property?"

He types. "Do you want to manage it?"

Ding: "Might be a good project for you. You need some responsibilities."

Phillip tucks the phone in his pocket. He sits quietly. He takes the phone back out.

Typing: "How's she doing?"
Ding: "You should ask her."
Typing: "I intend to."
Ding: "Sure."
Phillip rolls his eyes.

A thump, loud enough to be heard from the curb, angry but impotent with distance, comes from the house. Phillip turns and catches the drapes settling in a third-floor window. The real estate agent comes out the front door, talking on his phone. He looks up, then back into the house, confused. He continues talking and pulls the door closed behind him.

The street is empty, and there is no wind in the leaves of the poplars. Phillip rubs his neck again, sighs. He taps his phone, puts it to his ear, waits for an answer, and says, "Hi, Mom."

MOURGADZE

Cameron MacDonald

Cameron MacDonald *is a master's student living in Toronto. When not writing, he spends his time learning Gàidhlig, playing tennis, and supporting terrible sports teams.*

Mourgadze

In my two years working at the sprawling university library, I learned four truths. The first is that books smell the way they do because of mould, rot, and worms, not because they hold ancient wisdom. The second is that university students can sleep absolutely anywhere. The third, in the same vein, is that university students can hold amorous congress absolutely anywhere. The fourth is that, despite the beleaguered firefly of intelligence buzzing around the hollows of their skulls, university students have an unparalleled penchant for leaving their things behind. On the carpet, on the shelves between books, on the chairs, on the tables, hanging from lamps, and even — just once — on the back of a toilet. Their favourite spots, though, were the numerous study holes scattered throughout the library, mostly on the upper floors. They were soundproof rooms tucked into the darkest corners of the building, with lockable doors and no windows. The university official who greenlighted this particular architectural feature, given truths two and three, must have been a veritable mastermind.

As the youngest employee, and, incidentally, the only one capable of navigating the upper floors without need of a stair lift, it was my job to scour the library at the end of each night with an empty cardboard box, two latex gloves, and a small yellow bin meant for biohazardous waste.

It became a game. How many calculators richer would I be? How many pens could we add to the pen drawer? How many rabbits could I find trying to spend the night in the reading holes? How many watches could I keep in the lost and found for six weeks before my morals took a sabbatical and I sold them online?

This evening, though, I made an unusual find.

It had been a slow night of treasure-hunting: two pens, one of them chewed; many pieces of scrap paper; several coffee cups in varying stages of emptiness; and a three-ring binder with only two rings. All the typical nooks and crannies had been empty, which I attributed to my fastidious nightly cleaning and the thinly veiled aggression I hurled at anyone who seemed primed to set up camp or to litter. I knocked on the door to the last reading hole on the third floor and popped in the master key without waiting for a reply. The door came open without a creak or a groan, and I prepared myself for all manner of ghastly prizes: a spilled spice latte, a melted chocolate bar, a spent sausage wrapper from a romantic evening.

Instead, what I found was a small wooden cube on the floor beneath the table, leaning crookedly against one leg of a chair. I recognized it immediately as one of those Japanese puzzle boxes you see people trying to solve on YouTube. It felt heavy in the hand, unbalanced. Its side panels were arrayed in a complex tessellation of squares, weaves, and triangles. I was by no means a wood expert, but I recognized the distinctive colours and grains of walnut, cedar, maple, and oak. A fine piece, certainly, and one that would be missed by whoever had dropped it midway through their study session and left without realizing they'd lost it.

I popped it in the cardboard box with the rest of my finds, finished my combing of the stacks and the remaining study holes, and made my way back down to the main floor.

"Anything interesting tonight?" asked Owen from behind the information desk. He was peering through his comically tiny spectacles at the computer screen, his lips pinched like the top of a drawstring bag.

"Actually ..." I plonked the puzzle box on the desk in front of him.

He frowned at it. "What is that?"

"A Japanese puzzle box."

"Huh." His fingers fluttered away on the keyboard. "Isn't that pretty?"

"Can we put it in the valuables drawer?"

"Why, honey? Can't be worth that much."

"Well, I don't know about this one, but I've seen some online that go for five hundred bucks."

He regarded me coolly over the rims of his glasses. "You're kidding."

"No. Seriously. Whoever lost it will definitely come back for it."

"Gosh," he said, placing a hand on it. "I suppose they will."

I smiled at his enthusiasm as I distributed my haul into piles: paper, plastic, waste, lost items. "Think you can solve it?"

He gave it a few raps with his knuckle. "I don't see any seams."

"That's the point. You have to slide the panels or spin the box or shake it or something. Each one is solved differently. It's cool. You can hide stuff inside."

Owen inhaled loudly and said in a small voice, "*I wonder what she's hiding.*"

When I returned to the front desk after doing my final closing duties, Owen was still fiddling with the box. "Any luck?"

"No." He ran one hand through his coiffed salt-and-pepper hair and sighed. "Does it come with a mallet?"

I raised an eyebrow.

"You try, then."

"Owen, it's almost 4 a.m. If I touch that thing, I'll be here until we open again."

"What if someone comes back for it tomorrow before you're in and you never even get to try?" He wiggled it in the air.

I pursed my lips and checked the clock. "Okay. Just ten minutes."

"Good girl."

True to my word, I stopped after ten minutes, then tucked it with some reluctance into the locked valuables drawer along with the jewellery, credit cards, and foreign cash. I had tried all the moves I'd seen done on YouTube; spinning, knocking, shaking, rattling, smacking, rubbing … with no luck.

"It's like crack," I conceded under Owen's sympathetic gaze.

"*Love* the Japanese," he agreed.

Nobody came back for the puzzle box. It was there when I came into work the next day, and again the next day, and again the next. Every day, when I had a minute free, I would have another go at solving it. Then half an hour at lunch. Then fifteen minutes on break. Then ten minutes at closing, then fifteen minutes at the next close, then twenty …

A week after I found the puzzle box, I found myself dragging my feet out the door at 5:00 a.m., torn between an almost rabid desire to solve the puzzle and a more sober determination to maintain my sanity and my sleep schedule. At home, though, I spent most of my free time researching puzzle box solutions. I encountered several helpful websites, PDFs, and YouTube channels. Every few days I would come across a new method of attack and I could hardly wait to go into work and try it out. It always failed.

Then, on my lunch break one rainy Tuesday, with a cracker halfway out of my mouth, I heard a tiny *cluk*. All the blood rushed to my eyelids, and I opened them wider than I ever thought was possible. With my thumb I placed a small amount of resistance on the panel where the small seam had appeared. I pushed upwards. The panel, with the smoothest, most soothing wood-on-wood sound, slid up by half an inch, revealing a solid interior panel of dark walnut. Imprinted into the walnut panel in gold inlay was the word:

MOURGADZE

After my initial euphoric paralysis, I felt myself deflate. Was that *it*? A maker's mark? No interior compartment? I gave the box a small shake and there was a quiet but definite rattle that hadn't been there before. Surely that meant there were more steps.

I pressed and slid all the other panels, I spun the box on every axis, I shook and I flipped and I smacked, but nothing else came loose. Perhaps I had to slide the first panel back into place before continuing? So I did.

I worked for the rest of my lunch break and even into my shift, but I couldn't make any progress. I couldn't even slide back that first panel to reveal *mourgadze* again.

"Any luck with the box, Soph?"

I looked up. Owen was standing at the door, prodding his fork into a Pyrex container of pesto linguine. When I explained my progress, he put down his lunch and came to examine where the seam had appeared, which was now frustratingly invisible.

"You can have another go at it if you want," I said, rising from my chair. "I need to do some re-shelving."

"Okay, hon."

I made my way out of the back room, intending to go towards the stairs, but I hesitated in front of one of the computers at the front desk. I typed quickly, cognizant of the hawkish eyes of the other librarians, and hit enter.

Your search — **mourgadze** — did not match any documents.
Did you mean: *mungadze, Maori adze, giorgadze, morgades?*

I narrowed my eyes and tried *mourgadze puzzle box*. After some initial hope when that search returned a few results, I soon realised that the search engine had automatically excluded the word *mourgadze* and had simply returned results for *puzzle box*. I saw all the links I had clicked in the past for my research. I clicked the "must include *mourgadze*" option and the page reloaded.

Your search — **"mourgadze" puzzle box** — did not match any documents.

"Are you sure you spelled it right?"

I jumped an inch. "Jesus, Owen!"

He snorted from the back room. "Sorry. There really isn't anything?"

"Not a website. Not a forum."

"Hm. You go do your re-shelving, and I'll see what I can dig up."

I found myself unable to concentrate for the rest of the day. I mis-shelved several books, went to wrong floors and wrong hallways, and completely missed an obvious flirt from a guy who, judging by his helmet-hair, was a hockey player, but was kind of cute despite that shortcoming.

I returned to the front desk on multiple occasions to ask Owen if he'd found anything, but each time he said he hadn't, and one time he actually got a little short with me, for which he later apologized. Then I apologized for having pestered him. But when Lorraine, hawkish librarian number one and my self-proclaimed 'superior', told me off for being distracted on the job and muttered something under her breath about millennials, Owen and I both flipped her off behind her back and it was clear our brief bout of tension had been erased.

The door to Dr Sempere Agut's office was squat and narrow, painted quite recently and quite cheaply. A tiny white line tracked a heartbeat pattern halfway around the base of the brass knocker, the product of one rebellious paintbrush hair and a disdain for, or ignorance of, painter's tape.

Taped on the door was a sheet of paper reading OFFICE HOURS, with the list of hours underneath it scored out in Sharpie and replaced in messy handwriting with "*by appointment, happenstance, or divine intercession only.*"

I let myself close my eyes for a moment and checked with my left hand that my bag was still over my shoulder, even though I could feel it digging into my skin, while my right hand brushed the hair from my face and scraped away any ghosts of my to-go lunch from the corners of my mouth.

I hadn't spoken to a professor in years.

I had intended to go straight to a master's after finishing up my undergrad but had missed the application deadline by about a month. In hindsight, this was probably divine providence; even if I had gotten into the program, I'm not convinced I would have lasted the full year. The concept of *mastery* was slightly overwhelming given that, for me, even basic competency was little more than a sputtering mirage in the distance.

My fingers, too disorganized to be considered a fist, hesitated in the air. I cleared my throat, wrapped two fingers gingerly around the knocker's cold ring, and tapped twice.

And twice again, when no answer came.

And once more, just in case Dr Sempere Agut was hard of hearing.

I emitted a very quiet "*hola?*" and gave up, spinning on my heel and dragging my feet down the corridor towards the elevator.

The elevator dinged, and out stepped Professor Sempere Agut.

"Professor!" I exclaimed, probably too loudly, and he looked up from the notepad he was scribbling in. His bag began to slough off his shoulder, and he shrugged it back.

"Sorry to bother you, Professor Agut. My name is Sophie Saha. I graduated from the Philosophy department two years ago."

He cocked his head slightly as if he weren't quite sure if I was expecting congratulations, but his smile was warm enough, so I continued.

"I work at the library. When I was clearing up the other night I found something and ... right. Okay. This sounds silly now. But I found a Japanese puzzle box, and I haven't been able to solve it."

He raised his eyebrows. "Do … do you want me to solve it?" he asked quietly. His accent was like butter.

"Well, yes. Sort of. It's just that, well … I didn't just pick you out at random." I squinted, hoping that didn't sound too cheeky. "I looked for solutions online, but I couldn't find any. And another librarian said you'd come in once looking for books on puzzles, so he suggested I come to your office to see if you would know what to do."

If he was aware of how awkward and rambling I had just been, he didn't show it. He simply stared back at me, his face pleasant and blank. I idly scrutinized his aggressively receding hairline and decided I didn't quite mind an aggressively receding hairline. "I do like puzzles," he admitted, shrugging his bag back onto his shoulder again and flipping closed his notebook. "Could we go into my office?"

"Oh, right, okay! Of course. Sorry, Professor."

"It is no problem." He placed his notebook on the ground so he could fiddle with his keys, and I briefly wondered if I should pick it up and hold it for him or if that would seem too meek. Before I could make up my mind, he had unlocked the door and kicked the notebook into the office. It spun along the floor and settled under the desk. "Apologies for the mess," he said, plonking his bag down in the guest chair. Then he realized that I would have to sit there, and he moved it onto the window ledge. He lowered himself into a leather chair that seemed to sink six inches under even his measly weight. I could only see his head over the desk. "What did you say your name was?"

"Sophie Saha."

"Nice to meet you." He held out a hand at shoulder level and smiled warmly. He *was* handsome, in an odd sort of way, despite the hairline and the crooked teeth and the wide-set eyes and the slightly hooked nose. And the air of absentmindedness wrapped about him like a robe. "You can call me David. If you are not my student, I am not your professor."

Nodding and smiling, I reached into my bag, grabbed the puzzle box in one hand, and placed it on the desk. "So this is it."

He raised his eyebrows. "Very beautiful. You are right to say that it is Japanese. This looks like a Karakur … hm. Mm. Maybe not." He reached out his hands hesitantly. "May I?"

"Of course."

He stroked it gently with a thumb, as if asking the box permission too, then took it in his hands and examined it with a furrowed brow. "Maybe not," he repeated. "Have you managed to open any of the panels?"

"Well. Sort of. I slid one back about half an inch but that was it. I just came up against a darker panel. It reads *mourgadze*. Do you know what that means?"

He moaned thoughtfully. "Possibly the signature. Can you show me how you got there?"

I clicked my tongue. "I … I'm not sure I can. I don't even know how I—oh."

The sliding panel made a tiny *cluk*. "Ah," said Professor Sempere Agut. He looked closer at the newly exposed walnut panel. "*Mouuurgadzeee*."

"It took me longer than that."

"Ah," he said again, waving a hand dismissively. "I do these all the time. You get to know the tricks. But, having said that …" He turned the cube over and over in his hands and looked up at me. "I have absolutely no idea what to do next." He spent another few minutes trying different solutions, most of which

I had already tried, and eventually he leaned back in his chair and placed the puzzle on the table. He gave me a few satisfied nods. "Where did you say you found this?"

"In one of the study rooms on the third floor. It was just lying on the ground. I think someone forgot it."

"And no one came back for it?"

"No. It's been over a week."

"Ahhh. What a shame. It is a handsome piece. Probably cost a *céntimo* or two." He looked back and forth from me to the piece, seeming conflicted.

"Would you like to keep it for a few days?" I asked, feeling a smile creeping onto my face.

He mirrored my smile, looking slightly relieved that he hadn't had to ask. "Are you sure no one will come looking for it?"

"If they do, I'll know where to direct them. How long do you think it'll take you?"

"Ohhh." He shrugged in a way that was so Iberian it nearly made me cackle. "Maybe two days. I only have one class to teach tomorrow, and I consider this research."

"Quite right," I agreed. "If anyone deserves to devote his time to worthless mysteries, it's a Professor of Philosophy."

He laughed deep in his chest and stood up, offering me his hand again. "Very good. Thank you so much for thinking of me, *Señora* Saha."

"Oh. I'm not married."

He gave a small bow. "*Señorita* Saha, then. Come back on Friday and I'll let you know if it's solvable."

"But you won't tell me the solution?"

He scoffed. "Please. I would never. Where would be the fun in that?"

He watched her through the window as she made her way across the road towards the library, her bag slung over one shoulder, her lazy chutes of hair bouncing around at the small of her back. With a long sigh he lowered himself back into his chair, plucked the puzzle from the table, and gave it a few sad strokes with his thumb.

There were a series of dull *cluk*s as he manipulated it in deft fingers. His expression was almost wistful as he slid the top panel from its position, slid the back panel upwards, and pulled out one of several tiny wooden drawers. He licked his pinkie finger with the very tip of his tongue, poked it in the drawer, and it came out with a small rectangle of plastic stuck to it. From his desk he retrieved a small black cell phone, which he opened with a pin, and a black diary. He slid the rectangle of plastic into the phone, replaced the back cover, and dialled a number from the diary.

The line connected after one ring.

"We have cause for concern," said the professor, exhaling. He rose again from his chair and began to walk towards the window.

There was a low, throbbing hum from the other end of the line.

"He left it behind in a library. In a study room. On the floor."

Another hum. A mumble.

"Yes. A girl. A librarian."

Another mumble. A question.

Professor Sempere Agut looked out across the street to the front doors of the library, where Sophie had stopped to chat to another young woman. He reached up with one hand to close the blinds, moved back to his seat, and sighed.

"Yes. Friday."

THE 2020 MAGPIE AWARD FOR POETRY

THE 2020 MAGPIE AWARD FOR POETRY

Intelligent and bold, magpies are playful birds. And like their avian namesake, this year's Magpies offered a nestful of smart, strong, and feisty contenders.

Thank you to Renée Sarojini Saklikar, our esteemed judge——and this issue's featured author!——for once again lending her talent and insights to the Magpies. Here's what she had to say:

First Place: 'they say you will teach me more than I will ever teach you' by Charlene Kwiatkowski

Kudos to the writer of this sweet sonnet: great tone and rhythm, and wonderful unity of voice and focus. Iambic pentameter(ish) is a true poet's feat and one of my favourites.

Second Place: untitled by Maria Ford

I admire ambitious, expansive poems, and we get that here with loads of interesting things. Great diction and imagery.

Editor's Choice: 'Hummingbird Elegy' by Cara Waterfall

This year's entries were so enticing that *Pulp*'s poetry editors (and first judges) Emily Osborne and Daniel Cowper just couldn't resist picking a charm for themselves: *Each short line in this elegy is like a prism's facet, reflecting the bright tones and soft sounds of tiny birdlife. But the poem also cuts like glass, balancing the fragility and terror of mourning.*

The 2020 Magpie Award for Poetry Shortlist

Kenna Bell for 'The Trajectory'
John Blair for 'On the Perseid Meteor Shower as a Metaphor
    for Joy'
Maria Ford for untitled
Helen Gowans for 'Crete'
Charlene Kwiatkowski for 'they say you will teach me more than
    I will ever teach you'
Erin McGregor for 'Even before I speak (a poem for my
    stepdaughters)'
Kat McNichol for 'The Road Between'
Jeff Parent for 'Mercurochrome'
Angela Rebrec for 'A series of opposing reflections in a house
    of mirrors'
Cara Waterfall for 'Hummingbird Elegy'

Charlene Kwiatkowski is a city lover living in Vancouver, Canada. Her poetry has been published in Train, PRISM international, Barren Magazine, Long Exposure, *and elsewhere. She has a master's degree in* English Literature *and works at a contemporary art gallery. You can find her blogging (when new motherhood allows) at textingthecity.wordpress.com.*

Maria Ford has authored poetry and countless other things since grade school. She holds two degrees in English Literature and has self-published two chapbooks. This year, you can find her poetry also published in Pangyrus. *She is currently writing a book of creative non-fiction / documentary poetry. Visit her on Instagram @progressivetense.*

Ottawa-born and Costa Rica—based, Cara Waterfall has work featured in Best Canadian Poetry, CV2, The Fiddlehead, *and more. In 2018, she won* Room's *Short Forms contest and second place in* Frontier Poetry's *Award for New Poets. In 2019, she was a finalist for* Radar Poetry's *Coniston Prize and shortlisted for the* CBC Poetry Prize. *She has a diploma in Poetry and Lyric Discourse from* The Writer's Studio *at SFU.*

*t*HEY SAY YOU WILL TEACH ME MORE THAN I WILL EVER TEACH YOU

BY CHARLENE KWIATKOWSKI

I could stay another hour
holding swatches up to the light,
debating the merits of Queen Anne's Lace
versus Candlewick, asking questions
like *will it match your crib?*
You, who will only care about milk
and comfort in the beginning,
blind to all colour except the dark
circling my nipple, a novice pilot
above a helipad, I teeter with the weight
of a hundred small things. I'm not asking
for Gloucester's or Tiresias's fate,
but just a bit of mud and spit —
a puddle-splashed shin, a baby's bib.

{UNTITLED}

BY MARIA FORD

think of agriculture as something the grasses did to people
as a way to conquer the trees.[1]

To survive at -60°C
Alaskan wood frogs concentrate their bodies
with cryoprotectant sugar
freeze solid until spring   breathless   beatless.
Tubeworms 8,000 feet under the sea
feed on hydrothermal toxins   deaf, blind
bags of bacteria[2] turning poison
into energy.
Red blood cells in the body of Andeans
work harder[3]   hematology for paper-thin air

organisms can get used to anything   thrive anywhere.

On the plains, winds can reach 140 kph
throw us into trees   buildings   tailspins on ice
we've all sworn we'd die that way   or swallowing dust.

Prairie grasses sway, bend, sigh
built for this.   You were
your mesmerizing dance adapted
to the worst conditions
your trick to grow from the base (not the tip).
Bite, chew, tug, mow   season after season
you burst up green again   tougher.

You had
volume, strength, girl-balls, hatred, anger
I offered   safety   parents   love.
We selected each other
our trick in the roots
12 feet under, deep and entangled
tapping water, holding each other
against the tug of teeth
holding the earth in place   stubborn

boys and men trampled above

8,000 y.o. children of glaciers
rooted in sediment, rain shadow
in winter we burrowed below frost (crystals)   in summer
trees burned above (charcoal)
we were self-reliant   pollinated on wind
pushing and pulling each other.
(Speciation) I drifted   airborne.
You with all the reasons to leave
dug in, burrowed deeper
your children born there

[1] Michael Pollan. Botany of Desire. 2001: "Our grammar might teach us to divide the world into active subjects and passive objects but in a coevolutionary relationship every subject is also an object, every object a subject. That's why it makes just as much sense to think of agriculture as something the grasses did to people as a way to conquer the trees."

[2] Molly Sequin. 'Frogs that can freeze their bodies and 6 other crazy ways that animals survive their treacherous environments' businessinsider.com/these-7-animals-have-crazy-adaptations-to-help-them-to-survive-in-their-habitats-2016-7#tubeworms-turn-toxic-water-into-food-6

[3] Hillary Mayell. 'Three High-Altitude Peoples, Three Adaptations to Thin Air'. National Geographic. February 25, 2004. nationalgeographic.com/culture/2004/02/high-altitude-adaptations-evolution/

Hummingbird Elegy

by Cara Waterfall

Because the skylight brimmed
Because the moon seemed
      to inhabit   this room
Because
   I could not speak your way
 to the open window

         The next morning
I had to gather
   your cramped legs —
        that mess
of pink yarn
    bound by spidersilk
       & ants —
   in my palm
& watch that inner snow fall
  behind the glasswork
  of your eyes

Last night
            you were a prism   thickening
                  into gleam
        a tiny turbine
                  of white flame
                                    & precise silences
            whose wings could singe wind
            whose beak was a rapier
            whose forked tongue   like a king tide
                        muscled toward nectar

Now the forest grows
                        inside you
                                    & your eyes
            are milky as sea-stones

I tried
        to be merciful
balancing your quivering body   on a frond
but your beak   tipped forward
            into the green throat
                                    of the bush

I dipped my clumsy fingers in
            & dug you out
                  your last screech
            a rosary of pleas

Around us
            the trees shivered silver
      as your breath
became fainter

I wanted you   to feel less
I wanted   to feel less
& when you were gone
                        I felt less
But not   in the way
                        I wanted

The lack of you   like
      the thin honour of violets
            growing over   a grave:
      a hint of colour
            that never comes close
                  to helping house
      love & loss

PULP Literature

Four awards for genre-busting fiction and poetry.

The Bumblebee Flash Fiction Contest

Deadline: 15 February

Prize: $300

The Magpie Award for Poetry

Deadline: 15 April
First Prize: $500

The Hummingbird Flash Fiction Prize

Deadline: 15 June
Prize: $300

The Raven Short Story Contest

Deadline: 15 October
Prize: $300

For more information visit: pulpliterature.com/contests

Short stories, poetry, and comics you can't put down.

CHIMAERA

Weiwei Xu

Weiwei is a Chinese-Canadian artist who loves to draw upon (pun intended) her diasporic heritage for inspiration while adding humour and sometimes fantasy elements to tell stories. 'Chimæra' is a story about gaining a new perspective on a culture you've been told you represent, but which you have never really understood — and then finding a way to resolve your identity as part of that culture. Weiwei hopes her work will resonate with anyone who grew up divided between cultures!

Chimaera
by Weiwei Xu

"China is a civilization pretending to be a country."
- Lucian Pye

I was born in Canada to Chinese parents.

My first language was chinese.

I forgot most of it when I started [pr]e-school - but I was [sti]ll loud' n' proud of [b]eing Chinese though!

Not everyone was as excited as I was about it, but that wasn't important to me.

In fact, I embraced being Chinese and it became a defining part of my identity. I felt like an ambassador of Chinese culture!

Then I visited China.

(Apparently I also visited when I was a toddler, but I don't remember so it doesn't c

I knew basic mandarin, but not enough to really speak and read sig

This place is weird. I feel like an alien. I can only pick
out a few words. I can't even begin to understand real
chinese culture beyond what a foreigner experiences,
how can I call myself Chin I'm like a cheap
imitation of a real Chinese person
point? Chinese school didn't prepare me
So much of culture hinges on language,

almost there.
grandma only speaks
the dialect, so no
mandarin ok?
(mom)

Wait, so I can't talk to grandma at ALL?

your mandarin sucks too?
so you'd be almost as
lost as me if you left
this town ...

But maybe there's enough room in China for me too.

THE SHEPHERDESS: VERSAILLES

J M Landels

When we last saw former shepherdess and budding entrepreneur Toinette, she had landed on her injured feet as a housemaid to the mysterious countess known only as Madame. Unfortunately, the unsavoury men who pursued her from the countryside found Toinette again, inflicted a bullet wound on her companion Henri, and forced the household to hurriedly leave Paris for what they hope will be safety at the royal court of Versailles.

JM Landels is torn between travelling the world to teach writing and swordfighting, and never leaving her idyllic farm in Langley, BC. Her debut series, fantasy bestseller Allaigna's Song: Overture, and the sequel, Aria, are available from Pulp Literature Press and Amazon. You can follow her adventures with pen and sword at jmlandels.stiffbunnies.com.

$\mathcal{T}$HE SHEPHERDESS: VERSAILLES

I eyed the waiting carriage with trepidation. When had carriages ever brought me anything but trouble? At least this one was empty of wine-soaked dandies and their dangerous friends. Henri opened the door, and we four women filed in. When he began to follow, Madame stopped him.

"Ah-ah," she said, wagging a finger and pointing upward.

"Maeve," he complained. "Will you make an injured man ride above?

"Henri," she replied with an edge of steel beneath her smile. "Would you have one of these ladies or me watch the road for brigands like you? You probably lose more blood shaving than you did today. On top or behind, it's your choice. Either way, keep your pistol primed and your sword loose."

Mathilde and Marie-Claire had settled facing backward, so I took the left-hand space beside Madame. It took me some time to determine how to sit, with my panniers and whalebone stays. *Bien sûr* Henri had to ride outside. There was no room for both his bulk and our skirts in the carriage. Just when I'd finally arranged myself, I heard a bark, and the coarse grey mass of Rafael barged into the carriage.

"*Mon Dieu!*" exclaimed Mathilde while Claire let out a disgusted noise. Madame, however, only laughed as Rafael turned himself around, leaving a path of hairs on our skirts, and sat between the knees of Madame and me, looking beseechingly from one to the other.

"*Non, Rafael!*" I hissed, and pointed out the carriage door.

His hopeful eyes fell, and he dropped his body toward the floor, thumping the carriage with his tail.

"Oh, tsk, he can stay," said Madame. "It's a long walk. But you must lie down," she said to him, pointing at the floor.

He complied, still thumping happily.

"The hounds around here get better treatment than I do," grumbled Henri, as he shut the door on us.

Instead of climbing up beside the driver or taking the footman's post, he untied Marteau from the rear of the vehicle and bridled him.

"*Allez-y,*" he said to the driver, and lifted his head to us. "Ladies, I may or may not see you at court." He kicked Marteau hard, making the horse shuffle to a trot on the rough cobbles. I leaned out the window.

"That's half my horse!" I yelled, as he retreated around the corner.

"Never fear," said Madame, laying a hand on my arm. "He'll clear the way for us. And we are not defenceless." She motioned behind her, and I twisted in my seat to see Sauvegarde's unsheathed rapier resting on hooks above the back window.

She opened the box attached to the inside of the carriage door and lifted out an ivory-handled wheellock. Somehow the presence of weapons did not reassure me.

Nonetheless our trip was uninterrupted save for a stop to water the horses and relieve ourselves. Whether that was due to fortunate happenstance or Henri's presence on the road ahead, I do not know. However, after almost three hours in the jolting carriage, held upright by wooden stays that pressed into my shoulder blades and kept me from breathing fully, I longed to be on the back of Marteau, jolting trot or no.

The white stone and scaffolding of the new palace had just appeared over the heads of the trees when we came across Henri leaning against one of those lush oaks while Marteau grazed a circle around him. Madame stopped the carriage and made us get out while Henri tied the horse to the back of the carriage. She fussed around Claire and me, adjusting our hair, smoothing our skirts, and pinching our cheeks. "Bite your lips," she ordered. Mathilde in turn adjusted Madame's attire. Finally Madame surveyed us. "*Bon,*" she said. "You must look your very best when His Majesty sees you for the first time."

"His Majesty?" Out of the corner of my eye, I could see Claire's face go white. "Now? Today?"

"Use sentences, Claire, lest you sound like a sheep bleating. Yes, today. One does not show up at Versailles without showing yourself to the King. It is extremely bad manners."

I should have felt enraptured as our carriage rolled over the gravel road and through the gates of Versailles. I had wanted to move up in the world, to make a place for myself in society, and how much higher than the King's new palace could one go? But it was too far, too fast. I was doing nothing but running from one peril to another, and though Madame had promised the court would be a haven from Sauvegarde and his friends, it was like taking refuge from a wolf by climbing the tallest tree in the land. The wolf could not get me here, but the ground would finish me just as surely if I fell from these high and tenuous branches.

Madame was still delivering instructions to us as the carriage came to a stop. She handed me a fan. "Carry it, but for the love of God, don't use it." On the trip, she had told us of the intricate language of the fan, but it would take much observation and many private lessons before I could use it without signalling inappropriately.

We stepped out of the carriage in front of the gilt-framed doors of the château, my heart a panicked moth trapped inside a lantern.

Madame lifted her skirts and approached the porter. "Please show my valet"—she waved a lace-draped wrist at Henri—"to my apartments."

As she swept through the open door with Marie Claire and me at her heels, she muttered under her breath, "Let us hope they are still mine." It was the first hint of uncertainty I'd seen from her.

We did not walk far, for we immediately encountered a queue of nobles who lined the triple-wide stair and trailed off down the corridor. Those who were leaning against the wall or sitting on a stair jumped to attention when we appeared, then relaxed, seeing just a threesome of women. Madame joined the end of the queue with a sigh and motioned us in behind her.

She snapped open her fan and flickered it by her neck. "*Le bon Dieu,*" she said to us, but in a voice loud enough for the bottom third of the stair to hear. "It has been a long time since I have been here—I would have thought the wait would have got better, not worse!"

The man in front of us pivoted on his square-heeled shoes, spread the skirt of his coat, and bowed.

"*Comptesse!*" he exclaimed. "I would know that sweet Hibernian voice anywhere. To what do we owe the pleasure?"

Staying in his bow, he reached out, took her hand, and kissed it before returning to his full height—which, even in heels, was only on a par with my own.

Despite his small stature, he was a dashing figure, with an immaculate blue silk coat that matched his eyes, a mid-length wig of perfectly set blond curls, and unusually white teeth behind a lopsided smile.

"Michel Boisvert," replied Madame with a matching smile. "How strange to find you at the far end of this queue."

"Alas," he said, hanging his head in mock shame, "this is what comes of oversleeping."

"Knowing you," she replied, "I would have thought you'd simply stay awake all night and sleep in the staircase till morning. What is so urgent you'd spend your day here?"

"Ah, well." He cleared his throat. "I'm seeking permission to marry."

Madame's eyebrows shot up. "You. *Mon Dieu*, I thought I would never see the day. But I ask again, why the hurry?"

He gave a little shrug with his left shoulder. "It appears I have a rival. He's due back at court today."

"It seems you've left it a bit late."

The same shoulder twitched again, and he gave a mock-rueful smile. "And when have you known me to be early for anything, *Comptesse*? But you haven't answered my question. What brings you back?"

She twirled her closed fan. "Why, I am responding to His Majesty's invitation."

"That ... request ... is two years old if it's a day. And you accuse me of being tardy."

"I was occupied. I'm sure His Majesty will understand."

The gentleman lifted an eyebrow that seemed to say, "One hopes so." The line of gentility shifted forward, offering him the lower step. He swept a perfumed hand in front of him. "After you, Madame."

"Why thank you, Michel. You are too kind." She picked up her skirts and took the stair.

"My pleasure," he replied as we moved past him to stay at Madame's heels. "Though in return, you must introduce me to your lovely companions."

I have been up and down that stair so many times now that I no longer notice the rank smell of urine combating the scents of over-perfumed courtiers with unwashed bodies. But that may be because my fan snaps shut by automatic habit, and in place I bring my pomander beneath my nose. Unless of course there is someone on that stair with whom I must converse, flirt, or snub. Then, alas, I am compelled to use my fan and smile through clenched teeth, trying not to waft too much of the pungent air past my face.

But that first day I had a fan I'd been instructed not to use, no pomander, and senses completely overwhelmed by the odours, sights, and sounds around me. I was puzzled, but too self-conscious to ask why this giant gilt palace smelled like a latrine. However, the answer became clear when a finely coiffed demoiselle in satin mantle gathered her lace petticoats around her knees, showed a glimpse of pale green stockings and pearl-embroidered mules, and urinated on the stair.

Marie-Claire and I glanced at each other in shock as courtiers on the stairs below her casually stepped sideways to avoid the trickle that seeped down to the next step. Other than that, no one reacted to this barnyard behaviour.

"Isn't there a jakes?" I whispered to Claire.

The man who'd given us his place on the stair overheard. "Why, there are closets all over Versailles, mademoiselle. But who would give up half a day's standing on the stair to use them?"

"Are there not even pots?" I demanded, outraged that courtiers had no more pissing manners than a sheepdog. As if in answer, a voice from the top of the stair called out, in exquisite genteel tones, "Mesdames et messieurs, would you be so gracious as to pass the pot?"

An equally civil voice replied, "Alas, M'sieur, the pot is full."

At that there came the sound of more piss, this from the noisy height of a standing man. I held my lavender-daubed wrist to my nose, trying not to let my gag reflex turn into full eversion.

Michel Dubois noticed, produced a lace-trimmed handkerchief from his sleeve, and offered it to me with a bow. "Mademoiselle."

I hesitated only a second. "*Merci, Monsieur,*" I said through the perfumed cloth I now held to my face.

"Alas," he said to Claire, "I came ill-prepared today and have but one kerchief. But I can provide this." He produced from his coat pocket a tiny orange, studded with cloves.

Marie-Claire curtsied and thanked him — clumsily, I thought. I eyed the orange. I had only seen oranges once before, at a rare St Stephen's fair, but had lacked the funds to buy one. I desperately wanted that small golden fruit and the spices it held, but thought it would be ill-mannered to barter gifts in front of their donor.

Instead I examined the handkerchief in between the trips it made to my nose, fingering the monogram and the lace trim. But even through the smell of urine and the attar-sweetness of the handkerchief, the smell of Claire's orange tantalized me. It was tied round with a pale-pink riband, ending in a loop which Marie-Claire passed over her wrist. I eyed it jealously, dangling there like an afterthought, and worked up the courage to ask about it.

"Tell me, m'sieur, where does one find oranges?"

There was a sighing shift in the queue as we all moved up a step.

"Ah, mademoiselle," he replied. "One *finds* them all over the palace. His Majesty's gardeners wheel orange trees out of the orangerie every day and back in every night. Finding them is very easy. Obtaining them, well, that is a little more difficult. That one" — he gestured to Claire's wrist and lowered his voice — "was a gift from a lady."

Heads turned toward us, then away, then back again, leaving me wondering what those lips were saying behind their fans and kerchiefs.

The line of people on the stair moved erratically. We stayed on the second-to-bottom step for what seemed like half an hour at least, then progressed three steps in a matter of minutes. In this jerky, uneven motion, the brightly plumed snake of humanity crept closer to the sun. And when I say 'plumed', it is only partly a metaphor. *Mon Dieu!* Aside from the colourful ribands, lace, cloth of gold and silk brocade, there were more feathers than in a hen yard on plucking day. But it was a simple white goose feather that caught my eye, and not because it was bobbing on a lady's headdress or a gentleman's hat. It was twitching at eye level, two stairs past us.

I craned around the Countess and the full-panniered skirt taking up the step above her, and saw the twitching plume was attached to a pen, which was scratching furiously in a leather book. I took a sideways step to get a better view of the owner of the ink-stained fingers. Tallish, thin beyond skinny, with an upturned nose and a mouth pursed thin in concentration, he was a caricature of a marionette from the fairground. His cuffs were as stained as his fingers, and his brown coat duller than the plainest piece of stone in Versailles. Who, I wondered, would dare attend the King dressed as this plain brown wren? Even his dusty black tricorne lacked a feather.

Perhaps, I thought, eyeing the stairs around the bend, the quill lived in the hat band when it wasn't otherwise employed as a writing utensil. It seemed rude to stare—although the subject of my attention was so deeply engrossed in his work he could hardly notice. So I turned around and whispered to my new acquaintance on the step below me, "Who is that?"

He leaned outward as I had done. "Ah," he replied, "that is His Majesty's current favourite satirist."

I didn't want to seem more of a country bumpkin than I already was, so I did not ask what a satirist was. Instead I replied with, "Did you not say earlier a lack of fashion was decreed an offense at court?"

"Mademoiselle," he replied, "for every rule at court—and for every law in the land for that matter—there are situations, and individuals, that are exempt. Make a catalogue in your head to detail them and learn the reason why. It will be the greatest education in both courtly manners and the law you can imagine. Jean there can dress like a starving artist because he is one. He can appear at court because His Majesty adores his words. If the crown paid him enough to dress more finely, he would no longer be the person he is, and his words might dry up."

"So he is underpaid in order to keep him writing. I see very little incentive in that."

"Well, he could refuse the King's commission. Then he would go from a starving writer who nonetheless thrives well enough to eat and afford shoe leather, to one in rags, or a gaol cell, or a pauper's grave."

"It seems cruel of His Majesty to treat his favourite so." I said this behind my fan — the one I wasn't supposed to use — for who knew at what level of speech treason entered?

"Oh la la, not at all. His Majesty would shower him in riches as he's done with his other favourites. No, dear Jean has chosen this happy, or unhappy, medium for himself. Only time will tell if he lasts longer than the rest for it."

I turned, more fascinated than ever by the starkly out-of-place figure two steps above me. At that moment, the queue moved and took him onto the landing where the stair turned. One more move would put him out of my sight, so I memorized his clean-shaven, slightly sunken jaw, and the long thin tail of his queue, tied with a frayed brown riband. His unfashionably straight-legged pantaloons were tucked into the most fashion-able thing about him: his crumple-topped, mid-calf boots. There was no vest under the worn brown coat, and his shirt was yellow with age and dotted with ink stains. Every other person on the stair, and every bit of decorated panelling on the ceiling, walls, and balustrade was more eye-catching than this narrow, drab man. And yet I could not take my eyes off his quivering goose feather until the line moved again and he disappeared around the corner.

When we were nearly at the top of the stair, a black-vested functionary came down to take names. He raised an eyebrow and looked up again when the Countess passed him her card. "*Madame la Comptesse*, it is good to see you again," he said with utter civility and a complete lack of warmth.

Her smile was equally correct and equally warm. "And you, m'sieur. Do carry my regards to your lady wife."

He bowed and continued down the stair, collecting cards and names.

"That one hasn't forgiven you, I daresay," remarked Michel Boisvert from the step below us.

Madame flicked her fan shut and then open again, but said nothing in return. I was opening my mouth to ask what that meant when I felt two gloved fingers on my wrist. I turned to Boisvert, who gave the barest slow shake of his head.

A few minutes later, when a courtier's jest a few steps below caused a ripple of laughter, Boisvert stood on his toes to reach my ear. "When the fan shuts, the question is closed."

I glanced at Claire, who continued to study the lace trim of her sleeve, and then at Madame, who was regarding the frescoed ceiling with a bored aspect. When the functionary passed back up the stairs a few minutes later, her expression didn't waver. We endured another rise up the stairs in this awkward silence before the functionary returned and bowed stiffly once more.

"Madame, if you would."

The smile that broke out on her face would melt the ice on a duck pond in January, and the curtsy she gave was slow and deep. "*Mais bien sûr.*" She stepped sideways out of the queue and motioned us to follow her.

We gathered our skirts and tried to appear dainty—a house-maid and a shepherdess dressed up in borrowed finery—as we ascended past murmurs, raised eyebrows, and fluttering fans.

Black-vest ushered us to a space at the head of the queue, in front of a large-bellied man with an unfashionably short wig. The look on his gouty face suggested a complaint would be forthcoming, until Madame turned and curtsied.

"My dear Hubert, how delightful to see you again. Please forgive our imposition, but one cannot say no to His Majesty, can one?" She continued without waiting for a response. "Allow me to introduce Marie-Claire and Toinette, fresh from the country."

His pockmarked nose swivelled toward us and he took one of our hands in each of his thick and sweaty ones. He kissed Claire's, then mine twice, and then Claire's again without releasing our fingers. I wondered if it would be rude to pull them back and wipe them on my skirt.

I was saved from wondering when the door to the King's chamber opened and a courtier bowed his way out. Madame took each of us by the elbow and spun us around to check our hair, dust our skirts, and pinch our cheeks. Black-vest announced us, and we were admitted.

I barely had time to take in the splendour of this new room—gold, red velvet, and ostrich plumes—and realize it was a bedroom, before Madame's fan rapped me on the wrist. She hissed, "Curtsy."

I did, sinking as deep as my thighs would allow, glad of the panniers holding out my skirts so my shaking legs were not evident beneath them.

There was a click of heels on marble, and I saw a pair of legs clad in white silk uncross to stand on their gold-buckled, red-heeled, satin shoes. The shoes came two steps closer, bringing the shapely calves, riband-tied knee breeches, and a lace-cuffed hand into view. The hand extended toward Madame, and in the top of my vision I saw her bend to kiss the ring.

Then the hand moved right, toward me. It was a small hand, delicate even, especially compared to the swollen one that had grasped mine a mere minute ago. This one was scented with a complex mix of perfumes I couldn't identify, and a hint of orange blossom. It was nearly as white as Madame's.

I was afraid to touch it, so I brought my own hand just beneath it, and my lips touched the spiky gold of the ring. The fingers closed on mine — they were surprisingly warm — and lifted, so I had no choice but to stand. Then, most surprising of all, His Majesty turned our hands over and kissed mine, his moustache tickling my knuckles and the long dark curls of his perfumed wig brushing my wrist.

He dismissed me with a motion, and I stepped backward and sideways, unsure where to go. He repeated the process with Marie-Claire, then returned to stand in front of Madame, who was beginning to tremble from folding her curtsy.

"Catrin," he said at last, "do not think that bringing two beauties like these to court is enough to bribe me anymore. What am I to do with you?"

"Oh, there you are! *Enfin!"* cried Mathilde as the Countess, Claire, and I entered Madame's apartments on the upper floor of the palace's north wing. The November wind was blowing cold mist through the rooms, and the small fire in the hearth did nothing to abate it. Mathilde, however, was ruddy-cheeked and glistening with sweat.

"Claire, Toinette, fold those." She pointed to heaps of sheets, no doubt recently pulled from the furniture. "And then unpack the linens and make Madame's bed."

Madame kicked a crumpled drop cloth away from the settee and sank into it. Her pale complexion was whiter than usual, her normally full lips pressed to a wan line. "The bed first," she said with none of her usual lilt. "I am tired."

Claire and I glanced at each other and then Mathilde, who gestured wordlessly to the doorway on the right. We picked up the heavy linen chest and carried it into the bedchamber. The postered bed was still draped in white sheeting, which we pulled off in a cloud of dust. Then we set to rehanging the green brocade bed curtains folded underneath.

The meeting with His Majesty had not gone the way Madame had hoped, that much seemed clear, but I was unsure what exactly had transpired in the audience, even though I had been there the whole time.

When he had finally raised Madame from her curtsy, the King had seemed gallant and kind, but his words were loaded.

"It is far too long since you have graced the court, Catrin. What brings you back at last?"

She had dipped her head, unable to meet his eye. "Your Majesty, you know nothing short of dire circumstances could keep me away."

"*Ma belle*, were your circumstances so dire you could find no friend to aid you here?" He didn't seem to want an answer, for he continued. "But past is past. I am glad your situation has improved."

She dipped her head again. "It has changed, Your Majesty." I could feel she wanted to add 'not for the better'. For how could it have, given Sauvegarde's attack?

He waved his hand. "Very good. Then I shall see you at dinner tonight."

She curtsied. "I thank you, Your Majesty." She glanced at each of us. Taking our cue, we curtsied and backed toward the door.

"However," he added, "make sure you attend Monsieur Colbert first."

She paused a half breath in her retreat but otherwise did not falter. The colour, though, had drained entirely from her face.

As Claire and I tucked the bed sheets under the head of the mattress, I whispered, "Who is Monsieur Colbert?"

She shook her head. I couldn't tell whether that meant she didn't know or didn't wish to speak. As we finished turning down the bed, there was a commotion from the central room: the door opening and slamming shut, accompanied by a heavy tread that could only be Henri's.

"*Mon Dieu!*" he exclaimed. "That stable yard has doubled in size but tripled in occupants."

"Henri," moaned Madame. "*J'ai un mal de tête* — keep your bellow below that of a rutting stag, please."

I walked back into the room as Henri settled himself with a dusty thud in an armchair that barely encompassed his girth. His voice was not appreciably softer as he said, "The carriage is parked here, but I've taken your horses to the livery in the village. Else it would cost a fortune." He glanced at me. "You owe me a *pistole* for stabling your beast, *mademoiselle.*"

I picked up a corner of the dust sheet nearest me and walked backward as Claire took the other end. "I seem to recall," I replied as we folded the sheet, "he is half your horse, m'sieur.

And since you've had the pleasure of using him of late, his stabling falls to you."

We snapped the sheeting tight, and Madame clutched her head, rising. "Mathilde," she called to the housekeeper, who stuck her head out from the door of the left-hand chamber, "I must be up and dressed by four. Marie-Claire," she finished, and my sheet-folding partner disappeared into the bedchamber to help our mistress with her stays.

Mathilde had gone back into the other chamber, so I tossed the ends of the next drape to Henri.

"I'm not a maid," he grumbled. He stood with a great moan, clutching his side.

"Nor I," I answered, "but thanks to you, here I am instead of selling my wares in a Paris market."

"You mean here you are instead of raped and left in a ditch." Nevertheless he matched his corners of the sheet with practised ease.

We both turned the sheet the same way, and I had to swap hands to avoid twisting it. I walked forward, passing him the matched ends and retreating with the folded middle. "And yet I seem to be in peril from one minute to the next anyway." Having found the midpoint, I returned. "Who is Monsieur Colbert?"

He stopped, puzzled, then took the folded sheet from me. "Why, the minister of finance, of course."

The Countess's apartments consisted of three rooms: a central parlour, Madame's bedroom on the right, and another on the left. When the sheets were folded and stacked, I went into the left-hand room to see if Mathilde needed help. Henri followed.

"Mathilde, good woman," he announced, "no need to fuss on my account—the room is quite adequate as is. He sat on the edge of the partly made bed and extended one leg.

"Mademoiselle, would you be so kind? My side still pains me a great deal when I bend over."

I eyed his spattered boots, wondering if I was really obliged to touch them, when Mathilde tossed an iron bootjack from the hearth. It landed with a dusty thud on the carpet as he retracted his other foot in tempo.

"Take that with you as you kindly remove your boots in the parlour."

He snagged the bootjack with his toes and brought it closer, but didn't rise. "You ask too much of a wounded man who has ridden from Paris, Mathilde," he said, pulling his feet out of the travel-stained boots. "Now if you'll excuse me, I need a small rest." He lay back on the bed and extended his stockinged feet — only slightly less filthy than the boots themselves — out upon the fresh sheets.

With the broom she'd been using to gather cobwebs, Mathilde gave those feet a mighty smack. "*Sâle bête!*" she shouted. "Out with you. Those *were* clean linens. *Allez!*"

Henri recoiled his large body with remarkable speed, rolling to his feet.

There was something dangerous in Mathilde's eyes that went beyond dirty sheets. "How dare you settle yourself in Madame's apartments like you have some god-given right to park your large corpse anywhere it pleases you? Has Madame invited you to stay? Has she asked me to prepare a bed for you? *Non.* And until she does, this chamber is for us women, and you are not welcome."

He began to back out of the room, hands raised in mock — or perhaps genuine — alarm. "Your pardon, mistress. It did not occur to me — "

"Of course. It never does." She made the motion of spitting, though I noticed nothing landed on the carpet.

Henri skulked from the room, leaving his boots behind. Mathilde hurled them after him and slammed the chamber door.

"I'm so sorry, Mathilde," I began, brushing the mud and dried manure from the bed sheets. I didn't know why, but I felt oddly responsible for Henri — as if he were some giant child of mine who had misbehaved.

Mathilde threw her arms into the air. "Why are you sorry? That lout has been causing trouble since long before he brought you to us. Just like all the damned men in our lives." She paused, wiped at her eyes with her forearm, and resumed her usual busy-ness, though she hadn't done talking. "It's as if we don't exist till they want us," she said. "Did he think he could take the other room for himself, while we slept in the parlour or moved to the servants' quarters?"

Still not sure why I was defending him, I said, "I don't think he thought about it at all."

"*Et ça, c'est la probleme exacte!*" she said, flicking the sheet vigorously and jamming it with a vicious stabbing motion under the mattress. "It is beneath his notice — and any man's — to even consider where we might live when we're not in sight and being useful. How a woman lives from day to day is an enormous secret. We know all about their lives — their fighting and gambling and whoring. Their gallant acts when it's time to rescue us from some obvious peril, and their cowardly whinging when faced with the *rhume* or a spot of gout. Try giving birth sometime — now that is worth crying over."

This was obviously more than an argument over beds if it set the normally taciturn Mathilde off, but I didn't inquire, only listened.

"But the little things—being careful of what you wear and how you speak; being demure instead of strident or coquettish, sweet and sunny instead of aloof or cold. Any one of those things is enough of an excuse for a man to slide his hand under your laces and say, "Your mouth said '*non*', but your eyes, they said '*oui*'."

At this point Claire came into the room, closing the door softly behind her with a finger on her lips. "Madame is asleep," she said. "And so is Monsieur Dupin—on the settee."

Mathilde lowered her voice but continued talking—not to me, but to the door behind Claire. "And now Madame will have to justify her actions to that infernal man."

Claire came to Mathilde and put her arms around her with a heretofore unseen tenderness that shocked me as much as Mathilde's outrage had. "Sh, Maman," she said. "We will survive. We always do."

I eventually left Mathilde and Claire in the chamber—our chamber, I supposed. I felt an intruder in there, even though it was ostensibly my room too. Henri was sprawled across the settee, which barely continued his snoring bulk.

There was nowhere else to lie down, but I dragged one armchair across from the other and, kicking off my dainty but painful shoes, laid my aching feet on one chair while the other accepted the rest of me.

The hours standing in line had made my injured ankle swell like a sheep's bladder, and even elevated it throbbed in time to the pendulum of the clock Mathilde had unpacked, wound, and placed on the mantel. I wanted another pillow to get my feet higher, but they all appeared to be under various pieces of Henri's anatomy, and I lacked the energy to get up and extricate one.

I closed my eyes, but the rhythmic tick of the clock and the syncopated wheezing and sawing coming from Henri conspired against my attempts at repose.

Finally I opened one eye and glared at Henri. He was serene and untroubled by my baleful gaze, though his fingers twitched like farrowing piglets.

I wondered if the letter opener that had caused this trouble was still hidden behind his belt, which was, I noted, undone, no doubt to let his great belly breathe easily.

Despite my throbbing foot, I eased myself out of the chair and tiptoed barefoot across the soft, still cold carpet.

His snoring and twitching remained unchanged as I bent over and lifted his massive hand, letting it down gently to rest, palm up, on the floor. The fingers spasmed twice, but the snoring remained constant. It was a far simpler matter to fold back the buckle tongue of this belt, slide the strap end free, and let the buckle fall open, revealing the letter opener still snugged to the inside of the leather with cord. Unwrapping the thread took some time, but once it was loose enough, I slid free the letter opener and loosely rebuckled the belt before backing toward my chair.

Settled again with my feet up, but still cursing the lack of pillows, I turned the small knife over in my hands. It revealed no new information—except that I had seen the same sigil of sun and interlocked 'L's throughout the palace now.

Why did Sauvegarde have it, why did Henri steal it, and would there, I wondered, be some reward for returning it to its rightful owner?

I searched beneath my skirt and tucked it into the top of my hose, cinching the ribands tighter. Madame's writing box had come with us from Paris and was sitting unopened beneath the large, glazed window. With the stealth and concentration of a wolf bellying through the grass, I made my way to the box and opened it to find not one but two letter openers. We had packed in such a hurry, she would surely not remember having packed them both ...

With one of Madame's letter openers wrapped with thread to the inside of Henri's belt once more, I sat back in my chair.

"Henri," I said, then repeated it more loudly when his snoring still did not cease. Finally I picked up my slipper and tossed it at him. It landed on his stomach, which caused him to pick his hand off the carpet to bat at it, but the snoring continued. With the one slipper left in my arsenal, I aimed at his face. This brought some disgruntled sounds like those of a boar digging in the woods, and he flung an arm over his face. Otherwise, he stayed put.

"Henri!" I hissed, as loudly as I dared. At last I got to my weary feet and hobbled over to shake his shoulder.

I may have mentioned before that Henri could move extraordinarily fast for a large man. His great brown hand shot out and enveloped my wrist, twisting it away and causing me to yelp.

"I heard you the first time, mademoiselle. What does it take to get you to leave me alone?"

He rolled to sitting without letting go of my wrist, which made me twist sideways as he turned my elbow like a door handle. It brought our faces uncomfortably close.

"Let go of me!" I spiralled my wrist out of his grip, not feeling at all sorry when it bounced across his nose *en route*.

"Gladly." He rubbed his nose. "What emergency has you robbing me of sleep this time, mademoiselle?"

"Answers," I replied, massaging my wrist as I limped back to my chair. "Who is Sauvegarde, and are we any safer from him here than in Paris?"

"Of course you are. You think a man can walk in here and abduct a girl against her will under His Majesty's nose?"

"It's a big palace. His nose can't be everywhere."

Henri smiled. "That's why I like you—you're sharp of wit for a shepherdess."

I glared, though he seemed no more affected by my evil eye now than he had been when asleep.

He continued. "No, it can't. But his musketeers' noses are, along with many others. It is a crowded place, where everyone watches everyone else. And I suspect Sauvegarde is wary of coming here."

"Because of the letter opener?"

Henri nodded. "His Majesty is not known for giving away his personal effects, except sometimes to his mistresses. So there are three ways Sauvegarde might have come by it: one, he stole from the King; two, he stole from the King's mistress; three, one of the mistresses gave it to him. Any of these cases spell danger to him, and danger to anyone in possession of the item in question."

It took all of my strength of will not to let my hand steal to my thigh, where the letter opener rested in the top of my stocking. Instead I made a show of brushing imaginary dust from my skirts.

"You must excuse me," I said. "It is time to wake Madame."

I bustled past Henri, feeling the riband holding my stocking sag under the weight of the letter opener, and rapped on Madame's door. Without waiting for an answer, I opened it and slipped inside. I rested with my back against the door for two quick breaths, saw Madame had not yet stirred, then fished beneath my skirts to retrieve the slim piece of metal. Though it was only the temperature of my leg, it seemed to burn my hand. Why hadn't I gone to the chamber where my clothes were? I could have just put it in my chest. I hid it away again, this time between my chemise and stomacher, where it nestled between my breasts like the strongest piece of whalebone in the palisade of my corset.

I took another two breaths to recover myself, and then crossed to the Countess's bedside. "Madame," I whispered, then repeated it, a little louder. I leaned over and gave her shoulder a small shake, and then a larger one. "Madame?"

Her head lolled on the pillow, and a dribble of saliva trickled down her cheek. There was an odd smell in the air, like roses and apples, but sickly.

"Madame!" I shook her in alarm this time, touched a hand to her cold throat, and screamed for Mathilde.

It was Henri who barged through the door first. He grabbed my wrist and yanked me aside. Mathilde and Claire came seconds later.

"She's … she's dead!" I stuttered to their wide-eyed faces.

"No," said Henri, his fingers resting on her throat, "but very close to it."

As he had done to me, Mathilde yanked him away.

"Poison," I said, not knowing how I knew. "But how?" I turned to Claire, who was the last one in the room.

"Never mind how!" Mathilde was slapping Madame's face, trying to revive her. My mind whirled. *How* was important. When a sheep sickened, you needed to know what type of plants it may have eaten.

"Fetch a surgeon," Mathilde shouted at Henri. "Go, you useless lump of a man!" she added when at first he didn't move.

She picked up Madame's wrist and began rubbing it. Feeling useless, I ran to the other side of the bed. "Claire, rub her feet," I said. The midwife had done that when my littlest *soeur* was born with lips as blue as Madame's were now.

I reached the far side of the bed and picked up the Countess's hand. As I did, the studded orange pomander Claire had received from Michel Dubois rolled out of her palm and onto the floor.

Claire and I stared at it, and then each other.

"She asked me for it," Claire whispered. "To help her sleep."

I looked down at the hand I was holding, and saw in the heel of the palm a tiny, dark-red dot, no bigger than a pearl on one of Madame's slippers. I lifted it to my nose. The strange scent was overpowering.

I leaned over, feeling the letter opener slide against my breast — the least of my concerns now — and picked up the pomander by its riband. What devil would have cause to poison Madame? It swung on its cord, twirling slowly. There, amid the brown floret heads of the cloves that were pushed to their hilts in the orange, was a spot of redder brown that matched the one on Madame's palm. From its centre, like a lethal stamen, rose a shiny, steel needle.

§

The Shepherdess: Versailles *will continue in* Pulp Literature *Issue 30, Spring 2021.*

THE ARTISTS

Ashley Rose Goentoro

Cover artist, The Faery Godmother

Ashley Rose Goentoro is a fantasy watercolour artist from Richmond, BC. Often based on folklore, her work features whimsical scenes of the Faery Kingdom including pixies, elves, and goblins, as well as the natural flora and fauna of magical forests. To peek further into the world of Faery, follow Ashley on Instagram @ ashleyroseillustration, or, to purchase prints and original paintings, venture to ashleyrosegoentoro.com.

The Faery Godmother is inspired by European and Celtic folklore. When a family welcomed a newborn into their home, it was customary to leave offerings such as apples, honey, and lit candles to appease the faery godmother. If the new parents tempted fate and neglected to warmly welcome the faery godmother, the child could be cursed. But if they treated her well, the baby might have a long and happy life.

Weiwei Xu

Artist, Chimæra

Weiwei is a self-taught Chinese-Canadian artist who loves to mix humour, Chinese culture, and fantasy in their work. Weiwei has a degree in Life Science, which, while not particularly useful, occasionally manifests in their creative work and in their hobby of indulging in the drama of obscure scientific papers. When they are not drawing, they can be found running on local forest trails, making noodles, deep-diving into Internet rabbit holes, or playing tabletop games like Dungeons & Dragons. You can find more of their work at @peevishpants on Twitter, @itscoolguylink on Instagram, or theweiweixu.portfoliobox.net/home.

Mel Anastasiou
In-house illustrator
Mel Anastasiou loves drawing for *Pulp Literature* because she loves the stories she illustrates. She draws in black and white, working from imagination and inspired by details from Renaissance compositions. You can find more illustrations, as well as writing tips and news about her books and novellas, at melanastasiou.wordpress.com, and see her artwork on Facebook at Bird and Branch Artwork.

HALL OF FAME

These are the heroes — the Patrons and Pulp Literati whose monthly support helped bring you this issue. Please lift your glasses and give them a rousing cheer!

The Shareholders
Rapscallion

The Brewers
Robin McGillveray

The Landlords
Adam Fout
A Bursewicz
Isabel Cushey
Dana Tye Rally

The Innkeepers
Ada Maria Soto
Margot Landels
Ev Bishop
Shannon Saunders
Roger & Anne Anastasiou
Kevin Harris
Gillian Gardiner
Megan Shaw
Susan Lefeaux
Megan Dahl

The Cicerones
Elsa M Carruthers

The Bartenders
Alana Krider
Richard Gropp
Ron Graves
Kristen Mah
Robert Bose
Victoria McAuley
Dave Wayne
Scott F Gray
Abigail Bruce
Dietra Malik
Anna Belkine
Katriona Greenmoor
Famille Bussières
AD Bane
KT Wagner
Michael Weckworth
Deepthi Atukorala
Margot Spronk
Margaret Elliott
Peter Halasz
Bjarne Hansen
Leny Wagner
Kain Stewart
Chris Olee
kc dyer
Kimberley Aslett
Jan Fagan
Ken Oakes

The Regulars
CC Humphreys
Marta Salek
Rina Piccolo
Emily Lonie
Jenny Blackford
Jain Cairns
Michael Barrie
Leo X Robertson
Kristene Perron
Akemi Art
BC
Miriam Zibkoff
Meredith Frazier
Heather Ane Wilkey
Catherine Levinson
Vera
Charity Tahmaseb
Alexander Langer
Jeffrey Parent
Marilyn Holt
Risa Wolf
Barbara Pengelly
David Perlmutter
Christine McCullough

The Clientele
Ray Hsu
Melissa Hudson

If you would like to join the ranks of these worthies, you can become a patron on Patreon at patreon.com/pulplit, or join the Pulp Literati through our website at pulpliterature.com/join-pulp-literati/.

Are you our next
writer-in-residence?

Applications now open
for 2022-23
Apply by Jan. 15, 2021

ucalgary.ca/cdwp

UNIVERSITY OF CALGARY
FACULTY OF ARTS
Calgary Distinguished Writers Program

MARKETPLACE

Books

Advent *by Michael Kamakana* · We thought we knew what the aliens wanted. Think again. · pulpliterature.com/advent

Allaigna's Song: Aria *by JM Landels* · The long-awaited sequel to the best-selling *Allaigna's Song: Overture*. · pulpliterature.com/allaignas-song

The Labours of Mrs Stella Ryman: Further Fairmount Mysteries *by Mel Anastasiou* · Trapped in a down-at-the-heels care home. You'd be cranky too. · pulpliterature.com/stella-ryman-and-the-fairmount-manor-mysteries

What the Wind Brings *by Matthew Hughes* · Epic slipstream historical fiction · pulpliterature.com/product-category/novels/matthew-hughes

The Writer's Boon Companion *by Mel Anastasiou* · Thirty Days Towards an Extraordinary Volume · pulpliterature.com/subscribe/the-bookstore

Bookstores

Book Warehouse · 632 Broadway W, Vancouver, BC V5Z 1G1 · 604-872-5711 bookwarehouse.ca

Myth Hawker Travelling Bookstore · Canadian authors · Canadian content · small and independent press · mythhawker.ca

Phoenix On Bowen · 992 Dorman Rd, Bowen Island, BC V0N 1G0 · 604-947-2793

Village Books & Coffee House · 130-12031 First Ave, Richmond, BC V7E 3M1 · 604-272-6601 · villagebooks@shaw.ca

Western Sky Books · 2132-2850 Shaughnessy St, Port Coquitlam, BC V3C 6K5 · 604-461-5602 · store.westernskybooks.com

White Dwarf / Dead Write Books · 3715 10th Ave W, Vancouver, BC V6R 2G5 · 604-228-8223 · whitedwarf@deadwrite.com

Conferences and Events

Surrey International Writers' Conference 23–25 October 2020 · Virtual Event · siwc.ca

Word on the Lake · May 2021 · Salmon Arm, BC · wordonthelakewritersfestival.com

Creative Ink Festival · May 2021 Burnaby, BC · creativeinkfestival.com

When Words Collide · August 2021 Calgary, AB · whenwordscollide.org

Wine Country Writers' Festival 24–25 September 2021 · Penticton, BC winecountrywritersfestival.ca

Do you have a **story to tell?**
We can help!

Dreamers is dedicated to heartfelt writing. Visit our site for:

- Therapeutic Writing
- Poems & Stories
- Content Marketing
- Creative Nonfiction
- Writing Workshops
- Contests & Anthologies
- Residencies & Retreats
- ...and so much more!

www.DreamersWriting.com

DREAMERS
CREATIVE WRITING

GEIST
Keep it weird.
Subscribe today!
go to geist.com/subscribe
or call 1-888-GEIST-EH
FACT + FICTION · NORTH of AMERICA

on spec
the canadian magazine of the fantastic
Expect the unexpected.
www.onspec.ca

MICHAEL
KAMAKANA
ADVENT
WE THOUGHT WE KNEW WHAT THEY WANTED
WE WERE WRONG

The Digest Enthusiast
Book Twelve
June 2020
Michael Bracken
Steve Carper
Tony Gleeson
Vince Nowell, Sr.
Rick Ollerman
John Shirley
Joe Wehrle, Jr.

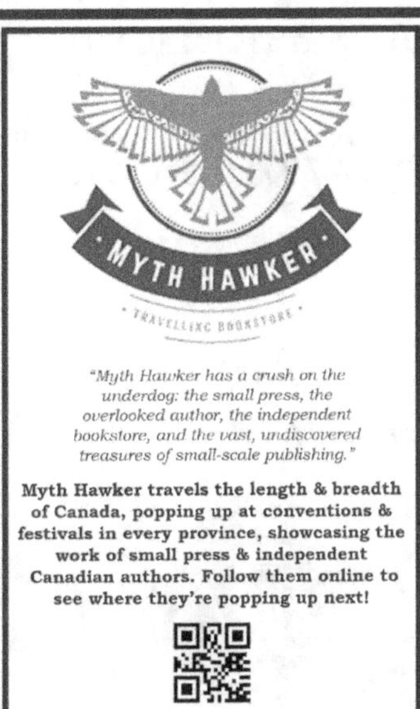
MYTH HAWKER
TRAVELLING BOOKSTORE
"Myth Hawker has a crush on the
underdog: the small press, the
overlooked author, the independent
bookstore, and the vast, undiscovered
treasures of small-scale publishing."

Myth Hawker travels the length & breadth
of Canada, popping up at conventions &
festivals in every province, showcasing the
work of small press & independent
Canadian authors. Follow them online to
see where they're popping up next!

www.mythhawker.com   @Mythhawker

JUNE 2020
MYSTERY WEEKLY
Magazine
Marshal Han was
wrong. Sometimes
evidence did fly
away...
Featuring
Tammy Huffman
Robert Lopresti
Arthur Vidro
Allan Durand
Luke Foster
Carl Robinette
Martin Hill Ortiz
THE CALCULUS OF
KARMA
by M. C. Tuggle

NEW FROM
PULP LITERATURE
PRESS

Allaigna's Song Aria

BY JM LANDELS

THE HIGHLY ANTICIPATED SEQUEL TO THE BESTSELLING

Allaigna's Song Overture

You can't escape magic when it's in your blood

pulpliterature.com

CONTESTS

Pulp Literature runs four annual contests for poetry, flash fiction, and short stories. For contest guidelines, prizes, and entry fees, see pulpliterature.com/contests.

The Bumblebee Flash Fiction Contest
Contest opens: 1 January 2021
Deadline: 15 February 2021
Winner notified: 15 March 2021
Winner published: Issue 31, Summer 2021
Prize: $300

The Magpie Award for Poetry
Contest opens: 1 March 2021
Deadline: 15 April 2021
Winner notified: 15 May 2021
Winner published: Issue 32, Autumn 2021
Prize: $500

The Hummingbird Flash Fiction Prize
Contest opens: 1 May 2021
Deadline: 15 June 2021
Winner notified: 15 July 2021
Winner published: Issue 33, Winter 2022
Prize: $300

The Raven Short Story Contest
Contest opens: 1 September 2021
Deadline: 15 October 2021
Winner notified: 15 November 2021
Winner published: Issue 34, Spring 2022
Prize: $300

ℬecome a Patron of Pulp Literature

By supporting *Pulp Literature* on Patreon with $2 or more per month, you will be laying the foundation for a secure future for the magazine, as well as ensuring that you never miss an issue! Your subscription includes four big issues of short stories, novellas, poetry, comics, and novel excerpts, delivered to your door or electronic mailbox each year. **Find us at patreon.com/pulplit**

If you prefer to subscribe through our website, go to pulpliterature.com/subscribe.

Or you can send a cheque with the form below to

Subscriptions, Pulp Literature Press, 21955 16 Ave, Langley BC, V2Z 1K5, Canada

Don't miss an issue!

- ❑ **Send me 2 years (8 issues) at the special rate of $90** (save $30)*
- ❑ **Send me 1 year (4 issues) for $50** (save $10)*
- ❑ **Send me 2 years of digital issues for $30** (save $9.92)
- ❑ **Send me 1 year of digital issues for $17.50** (save $2.47)

Name: ____

Address: ____

City: _________________________________ Prov. / State: __________

Postal code: _______________ Country:____________________

Email: ____

- ❑ Payment enclosed
- ❑ Bill me
- ❑ New
- ❑ Renewal

Make cheques payable in Canadian funds to J. Landels. Include email address for digital editions and Paypal billing, or subscribe at www.pulpliterature.com.

*for postage outside Canada add $20 per year in North America or $36 per year overseas.